SURVIVING

By

C.M.F. Kosai

ISBN: 1-4033-3094-8 (Electronic)
ISBN: 1-4033-3095-6 (Softcover)
ISBN: 1-4033-3096-4 (Hardcover)

Library of Congress Control Number: 2002105984

This book is printed on acid free paper.

Printed in the United States of America
Bloomington, IN

1stBooks - rev. 07/01/02

CHAPTER ONE

"Is Louis Ciparis a murderer?" I grasped the old priest's worn sleeve to emphasize my concern. Father Mary looked a little startled at my rude move. I did want an answer. I was putting my life in the hands of Louis Ciparis, after a fashion, and I had a right to know if I was traveling in the company of a murderer. I took my hand away from the man's sleeve as he began his answer.

Father Mary was a French priest. He was certainly different from any priest I would find in Boston. He had white hair and a shabby cassock, but there was no question he was dedicated. He was remaining in Morne Rouge to care for patients in his little hospital. He was staying here, in spite of the eruption. He was the kind of man who took his duty seriously. I guess in that regard he was much like a Boston priest and I should not laugh at his strange name.

His soft voice finally answered. "I don't know what his crime was." Father Mary shook his head 'no' and he paused giving this subject further thought. "It must have been serious," he finally continued. "He was in solitary confinement. I have no idea what he did. It is not important. What matters is God saved him."

"Isn't it ironic that the only person left living in the whole city, the only one of thirty thousand, is a condemned murderer?" I probed, still looking for an answer.

"I don't know that I would call it ironic," Father Mary replied. "God works in mysterious ways. I believe Louis was saved to do God's work. I do not know what his mission is, but he must have one. And I do not know that he is a murderer. Who told you that?"

"Your capresse servant, the one who brought me towels this morning, warned me to beware of Louis. She said he is a murderer, that he kills white men. You don't have any idea about his crime?"

The adrenaline started as I anticipated the trip ahead. My writer's blood felt the suspense of a good story working its way through my muscles and into my bones. My features on the aftermath of the eruption would be even better now. This was not just the story of the May 8, 1902, eruption of Mt. Pelee, or the destruction of the city of St. Pierre, Martinique, and all its inhabitants. There was a single survivor, one solitary man and he was mine to write about.

In June I had a tip there was a survivor. This led me on a hot, strenuous, never-ending hike from the ruins of St. Pierre up the mountain to Morne Rouge, skirting the still smoking volcano. Looking like an apparition myself, covered with ash and sweat, I finally reached the dust-covered village that resembled a ghost town.

The first thing I saw was the life-sized crucifix and the spire of the church standing solidly in the village. The houses were open and abandoned, with ash everywhere. Eventually I found Louis Ciparis in the care of Father Mary, the priest at Morne Rouge. I learned only the very old and infirm remained with the priest and this survivor. This solitary man, still living after the catastrophic eruption, was mine to write about. No one else knew there was a survivor of the hellish devastation. I marveled at my good fortune. Finding a survivor would turn this ordinary assignment into a jewel.

I smiled at the priest. "Whatever he did, Father Mary, finding the survivor here with you in Morne Rouge was something of a Godsend for me. Taking him to Fort-de-France for medical care, having so much time with him in the wagon going there and then your servant's warning on top of everything. It's too good to be true. This is the story a writer waits a lifetime for. Just incredible, isn't it?"

3

"Yes," Father Mary agreed. "Just remember, my son, this is a very special person. His doing God's work must be shown to the world."

Anticipating this agreement, I watched Father Mary intently. The flower-perfumed air and warm morning sunshine did nothing to soften the energy of my anticipation.

"Where is he anyway? What's the hold up?" My eyes wandered around the grounds outside the church where I waited impatiently with the priest and an even older mule.

It was a lush green morning. The palm trees were quietly weaving the scent of wild orchids around the vines that wrapped their trunks. A quick look revealed a bright spot of red hibiscus, but it was mainly a daylight tapestry of shades of green. What a good day for travel.

Father Mary pursed his lips. "I reluctantly gave permission for a voodoo priestess to perform a ceremony that is supposed to help Louis on the trip. I don't like the heathen voodoo of this island, but I know it exists. To keep in touch with these poor natives, to communicate with them, to teach them and save their souls. I feel forced to surrender to custom at times," Father Mary sighed heavily, as if ashamed of his own weakness before he continued.

"I wanted to wrap his hands and feet, but the priestess told me she would do it after the ceremony. There was no way he could walk. Two men carried him. They made a seat for him with their hands holding on to each others elbows, much like children do in play." He turned as something caught his eye. I looked too. It was Louis tentatively walking toward us.

Father Mary said under his breath, "I see she did wrap his feet and she must have done something to deaden the pain. He limps, but he can walk."

In spite of his age, Father Mary himself moved like a young man, with vigor and style. His face was unlined and his gray eyes usually sparkled mischievously. Only his white hair and shabby cassock gave him away.

"Louis may not survive the trip to Fort-de-France," continued the priest. "And this ceremony may help the natives cope with the final loss." He sighed again. "He is, as you say, the single living being from St. Pierre and to make up for bending my principles, this unwelcome subversion of my beliefs, I'm going to give him a rosary to help him on his journey. Maybe it will offset the evil voodoo."

Father Mary held up two rosaries. "One is for you Edward. Not to protect you from harm, but to comfort you if Louis dies before you get your story."

Father Mary chuckled to himself as he handed the rosary to me. "No, I should be kinder than that," the priest shook his head solemnly. "It is to remind you of this place, this little village of Morne Rouge high on the mountain, and my small hospital. I do hope you get your story. It will be a remarkable tale. God has saved Louis for great work and you are the agent that takes his message to the world."

I reluctantly took the rosary. It would offer me precious little comfort if Louis died, but Father Mary would feel better. "Father, you are too ambitious for me. I'll be happy with an award winning feature," I paused. "As I think about it, even if he is a murderer, I have nothing to fear. He's so badly burned he's too weak to kill a fly."

Father Mary answered quietly, "He's too helpless to kill an ant, poor man. He can't even feed himself. I'm truly surprised he's still alive."

As three figures approached our wagon I had to restrain myself from laughing. "Father Mary are you trying to show me that I'm responsible for transporting an angel? That's what Louis looks like with his flowing robe and straw hat halo."

"He was saved, so God must have something special in mind for him. Why not an angel?" Father Mary looked at me with some annoyance. "I am being practical. He needs protection from the sun, so this robe and hat make sense. Fortunately his face is not burned, so protecting it is easier."

The priest had bandaged the body of the burned man with strips of old sheets that could be glimpsed underneath a loose flowing robe. This made sense, as clothes would not be comfortable for the poor man. They would be too painful to wear. He was walking with his feet wrapped. His hands were also wrapped. Only the skin of his face was visible. He was wearing a wide straw hat to shield him from the sun.

Louis Ciparis, limping clumsily, accompanied by two old withered Creoles, cautiously approached us standing by the mule and the homemade wagon. It was painful to watch him move.

As the priest said, the young black man's classic face was not burned. At first glance he appeared physically strong and healthy, even handsome. The timeworn white cotton robe, softly flowing in the slight breeze, was unseemly for this tall man trying to maintain a brave posture balanced on heavily bandaged feet. His burns would not permit shoes, even if he owned any.

"Father Mary, how is he able to walk at all?" I whispered. "I saw his feet and hands. They were swollen and covered with repulsive yellow pus. He smelled like death."

Father Mary nodded, "I know." He called out to the slowly approaching man, "Welcome, Louis. It is good to see you walking."

"Father Mary," said Louis when he reached the priest, his soft voice still raspy from breathing hot air and ash many days before. "So, I never seen such a miserable cart like this. It looks to be an old weather-beaten wood box with skinny tree twigs at the corners to hold a canvas ceiling to the sky. And the little wheels, are they from bicycles? It is most very strange." Louis shook his head in wonder.

Father Mary was visibly hurt by the man's remarks. "Louis, I made this so you can lie full length on your stomach, or you can sit up, leaning forward on the special tray I added to support you. This wagon may look strange to you, but I'm very proud of my work."

Father Mary motioned toward me. "This is Mr. Edward Blake. He is the writer you met two days ago."

"So I remember him," said Louis with a glance at me. "Anyhow he is not the man who got so very sick and threw up when he come into my room." He turned his attention back to Father Mary. "So I think this way to travel may be good. Thank you, Father."

"Did that ceremony help you?" asked the priest.

Louis nodded his head yes and his lips formed a smile. "The priestess, she said I need great protection for the ordeal of this trip. She said for me this trip is most dangerous."

"Did they give you gris gris?" asked the priest.

"Yes, and a pacquet, and Clairin," Louis whispered back.

"Is the Clairin keeping you free of pain?" asked Father Mary with obvious disdain. Louis smiled at him, but did not respond.

"I have something much more powerful for you," Father Mary continued. The priest placed the necklace with black beads and a silver cross on top of the bandaged hand. "You know how to use this?"

"Yes, Father."

"Then see that you do."

Father Mary turned to me and confided, "I do think it best to go the longer route along the ocean. The shorter road on the ridge of the mountain is still in transformation from the eruption. You can walk the mountain road if you are healthy, but using a wagon makes travel strenuous. The longer trip through Marigot, is safer. It appears that Louis will not feel any substantial pain. You can thank the Clairin for that."

"What is Clairin?" I had no idea what Clairin was, but I could tell Father Mary did not appreciate Louis using it, even for medicinal purposes. "Personally I'm grateful for anything that controls his pain," I added.

"It a very strong unrefined native rum," answered Father Mary with distaste.

I nodded knowingly and offered my hand to the priest in farewell before assuming my place as the driver. After I got to my seat I turned to help Louis who was awkwardly climbing over the side of the wagon. It was obvious to me that Louis could not hold his body upright for the duration of the trip. His raw burns could not endure any prolonged exposure to the heat from the blistering rays of the sun. Even I noticed the pervasive heat rising as the sun climbed higher in the sky. Louis with his burned body would suffer dreadfully this day when the clairin wore off.

When we were both seated I said, "The picture we present, with the wagon and the mule, must be unusual to see. I hope this works. I've never driven a wagon before but I will ride at the front of this unique wagon and I will drive this pitiful creature Father Mary found somewhere and calls a mule. I swear I am determined do this," I said this with what I hoped was a reassuring smile.

"By anyone's measure the beast is not a healthy looking animal," conceded Father Mary. "He is old and skinny. He will plod along so slowly for you he will not raise any dust for you to breathe. He is too old to notice the chaos the volcano caused and too worn and tired to pay attention even to life itself. I am sorry, but it is the only mule I could find."

"I wonder why it's still alive? It seems so close to death. Father, you will offer special prayers for us to get to our destination won't you?" I did not believe the prayers of the priest could be much help, but it couldn't hurt.

"Of course my prayers are with you," replied Father Mary. He turned to Louis, "Because of the rain yesterday the air smells clean at last and that will help you breathe. No sulfur stink, only the aroma of wild flowers. It is a beautiful day for travel. Go with God." He stood back, waving us off.

There was a light layer of gray volcanic ash on the roadbed, but the mule, as slow as expected, hardly disturbed it. Even so, we would soon be leaving the tree-shaded grounds for the overlook where nature offered no protection from the sun above or the desolation below.

Father Mary watched us leave. We must have been quite a sight in our outlandish rig. We were two very opposite men slowly crawling away from him. We were the same height, same age, but Louis was uneducated and coal colored. I was well educated and white. What an adventure I expected. I couldn't wait to ask Louis about his crime, but I had to gain his trust first.

CHAPTER TWO

I shook the reins and the mule started to pull the wagon with a slow deliberate walk. "I certainly won't be able to speed this poor mule along. It's near death as it is. I'd better let it plod along at its own slow steady pace and hope we get to our destination sometime."

Louis smiled reassuringly at me. "That you cannot drive mule is fine with me, Mr. Blake. I never had such a wagon as this before and I cannot drive mules either. I also hope this animal lives to see us in Fort-de-France at the end of day. The Voodoienne says this trip is dangerous. Maybe that means I must walk when the mule dies and that would be painful."

"Yes, that would be quite painful. The cart is shaking with each step the mule takes. It may break apart before the mule dies. Whichever happens, we may both have to walk." I noticed Louis nodding his head in agreement.

"You don't know how to drive a mule, Louis? That surprises me," I observed.

"No, I do not drive mules. So why are you surprised? I am a fisherman. On land I walk."

"Louis, please call me Edward. There is no reason to be so formal in a situation like this. I want to get to know you." I studied the man sitting beside me. Louis appeared calm, tranquil and resigned. I was smiling to myself. "You look stronger than when I first saw you," I told him.

"So I am better and I did not need much help to walk. Two men helped me, but I could of done it with one," answered Louis. "My packages needed someone to carry them though, so they helped me."

As we reached the fork in the road to the north of he village I halted the slow moving mule before turning right to travel down the Eastern side of the island. I paused in consideration of the scene before me and proclaimed to Louis, "Isn't this view incredible! I'll never see anything like this again." I motioned with a sweep of my hand to point out the sight to Louis who had his head bowed.

"Just look Louis. Two bodies of water coming together, a smoking volcano and the ruins of St. Pierre." I smiled ruefully, shaking my head at the incongruity of the scene. "This is a remarkable place to see. I was so excited the first time I saw it. The cold Atlantic

Ocean, dark cobalt and mean and angry on one side. The warm azure

colored water of the Caribbean on the other. And now this," my hand

swept again over the gray lava-covered rocks of the ruined city below.

"Mont Pelee is still sending up puffs of smoke. She is demanding

attention, ruining the perfect cloudless blue sky. At least she isn't

destroying anything now. It's sad to see the remains of St. Pierre, the

city she destroyed so completely, so ruthlessly. But the ruins of St.

Pierre will remain a long time, and we had best get used to them."

"I hope this will be a successful trip for both of us. You will get

good medical care in the city. After all, Father Mary is out of

medicine. It also gives me a chance to talk to you and I am curious.

What was your crime that you were in solitary confinement?"

"So this I do not talk about." Louis snarled the belligerent answer

at me with surprising strength.

I drew back astonished. What happened to the soft-spoken badly

injured passenger? This threatening man was, indeed, a murderer.

Still, I knew if I could get Louis to talk, about anything at all, eventually he would tell his story. I would just have to start the interview at another place. I would persist.

"You told Father Mary that you were given things in the ceremony before we left. What is *gris gris*?" I asked.

Seeming serene and unruffled by his outburst a moment ago Louis answered calmly, "It is a charm to guard against bad luck. I could have used such a charm long ago, but they tell me not to be selfish. Because anyway it is lucky I live at all, even with a burned body. The *pacquet* is more important. It is for continued good luck and to help me." Louis reached into the wide sleeves of his robe and removed a black flannel bag from somewhere. "My *pacquet*. A conjure bag."

"What's that?"

It is good or it is bad. Either one. It casts evil spells or protects you and brings good fortune. It depends on what is in it. So mine protects me and makes me heal fast. You do not know about voodoo?"

"Very little," I confessed. "Much is good about it. So the priest does not think so. But I know. They gave me *clairin* so I feel first rate. I cannot walk to Fort-de-France, but my spirit is there already."

"What is so special about this clairin?"

"It is a rum drink we make at home and is not like what you drink. So you drink refined rum. This is a natural rum drink, from the juice of the sugar cane so it is clear and strong and always makes you feel good."

"The priest was telling me about *bamboche*. Do you know about it?" I asked.

"So that is what makes me voodoo. Anyhow the priest does not like it because he hates voodoo. He does not understand I have the church to believe in and to save myself forever, but the *bamboche makes* me want to live now. It is a party, a dance. Many people come and celebrate. It means nothing religious like a church. We drink freely and we love freely, any woman at all we can love during bamboche, if they say so.

"They call me a voodoo mystery sometimes. So it is my job to go around and get everyone happy. They have a good time and drink a little more, or love a little more. Perhaps to find another woman to make happy if they can.

"I like to party. What else is there? You work so you can party. I would like it better if I could just party and did not have to work. Don't you like to party?"

"I haven't had any experience with the type of party you are talking about. If it is an ordinary party, I can go or stay home. I don't much care. Why did the voodoo woman tell you this trip was dangerous?"

"I do not know, but my burns are not healed. So Father Mary thought I should stay longer, but he had no more medicine. He told me to go, but maybe it is not the right time yet." Louis said. "Let us talk about something else. Are you married?" asked Louis.

"No, I'm not married. Are you?"

"No. The woman for my wife is dead, unless she went away from St. Pierre for some reason. But I think she is dead. I have no family left. No one left. Everyone is dead to me so far as I know. So, no family, no friends, no work, no home, nothing. No joy, no reason for life, but I live. So I can walk a little and talk a little. I eat some, too, but I only exist and that is not living. I should be dead. I do not believe I should live, but I know it from the pain when I don't have rum. The pain is real."

I leaned my body away from Louis. I did not want the possibility of his pain rubbing off on me. I did not know what to say.

We sat in silence, bodies rattling, as we passed through fields of brilliant red and yellow flowers, untouched by the volcano on the other side of the island. Lush, life-holding, green grasses lined the narrow ruts we bumped over. The island colors were vivid and the warm breeze brought sweet smells of fragrant wild orchids. The perfection of the day soothed both of us in spite of the circumstances.

"You know Christopher Columbus called this the best, most fertile, most delightful and most charming land in the world. I agree with him."

Louis replied absently, "So who is Christopher Columbus?"

I should have known he might not know this. I answered, "He was a great explorer who discovered this island in 1502."

Louis looked away, disinterested.

"You know, I'm not from the island. I'm from the United States. I work primarily for a newspaper there," I told him trying to get more information from him.

"Father Mary said you were newspaper man, so I thought you someone important from Fort-de-France. How come you speak French so well?"

"My parents loved this island and brought me with them many times for holidays." I smiled at the happy thoughts of those visits.

"So why you taking me back? How did you get to Morne Rouge? Will you write about me?" asked Louis.

"I'm going back with you because I need to go to the city and so do you, and Father Mary feels he needs to stay in Morne Rouge—and yes, I will write about you, if you decide to talk to me. As far as I know, you're the only living person from St. Pierre after the eruption. I'll write about you and about what happened to the city. I'll tell people what it looks like now and how the people died."

"I am the only one?" Louis asked with a gasp. His eyes grew large and he drew back in disbelief.

"Yes," I gave the answer rather coldly, without feeling. It was a fact and he already knew his family was lost. There was no point in trying to soften the reality.

"You are sure? For certain?" Louis asked with a trembling lip.

"From everything I've learned, you are. Didn't you know that?" I waited impatiently for a response from the shattered man. At last Louis started talking again, sounding agitated and distraught.

"Father Mary told me the city was destroyed and most died, but I did not tell me that I am the only one who lives! No! I do not believe this! This cannot be!" Louis gasped for breath.

He finally appeared calmer and began to talk again, his voice growing raspy with emotion. "There are too many people in St. Pierre for me to be the only one left. There must be more alive from 20,000 people. You are wrong."

I answered very deliberately again, "I have been in Fort-de-France and interviewed a few survivors from a ship in the harbor. In Morne Rouge Father Mary introduced me to a man who saw the eruption from a distance. He was on the side of the city across from the harbor.

Father Mary himself saw the eruption and the destruction of the city and I talked to the men who rescued you.

"Also, I have been in St. Pierre and met a scientist there who told me what happened. He came from the village of Carbet. He told me there were two beside you. One, a man who hid in the basement of his house, was taken to Carbet. He is quite mad and not expected to live. There was a woman, a servant, also in a cellar. She died a few hours after she was found. You must believe me, you are the only survivor from the city and the city had grown from 30,000 to perhaps 50,000 people before the eruption."

"So this is why Father Mary says God spared me for important work, but I do not believe this." A subdued Louis shrank back into his robe. He continued softly, "Part of me does not want to believe Pelee erupted. I stumbled through the city so I know it did erupt. I was there. I know what I saw, but I do not believe it. I lost everything. It is not real for me. I do not remember plainly. Like a dream. It is not real. I do not want to remember this bad dream.

"Part of me knows the city is gone. Another part of me does not believe that. But when I walked through the city I did not see people or even buildings that were whole. Maybe I do not want to believe I am the only one left. Maybe I do not want to be the only one left."

After a long silence Louis asked timidly, "What does it look like now?"

"We saw it from Morne Rouge before we turned to this valley," I reminded him.

"I didn't look closely," he answered sullenly. "Tell me. What does it look like now," he demanded.

Louis looked bewildered. "When the men found me and brought me out of jail there was still some building walls standing. There is nothing now?"

"No. There was another eruption. Everything is gone."

Still trying to understand, Louis asked, "So what day was the eruption? Because I was in prison, I do not know what day it was."

"The first eruption was Thursday, May 8, 1902. That was the one before you were taken out of the jail. I think you saw some buildings then, but there was another eruption May 20."

Louis Ciparis laid his head down on the rim of the wagon in front of me. It was too much to hold his body upright. We rode on in silence for a while.

"It's beautiful here," I commented. "This is how I will remember the island here when I'm back home, without the destruction."

"Beautiful?" Louis asked. "I know this island and one other, which is the same as this island."

"It is beautiful, Louis. I have traveled widely, and this is a favorite place," I assured him.

"So I would like to travel someday, but I do not see how since I had nothing before and have even less now. I cannot even sign onto a boat to fish until I am well and strong. I do not know if I will ever will and be a man again. I will never be the same. Never be strong again. I love to party. Now that is foolish. So what should I be happy about? There is nothing to party for?" Louis dropped his head to the tray again.

"You are still a man, Louis, and you'll heal. It will take less time than you think. The sailors I met in Fort-de-France were not in St. Pierre itself. They were on a ship in the harbor during the eruption.

They were badly burned and they are healing very well. They will be going home soon." I tried to reassure him even though I didn't believe it myself.

"So, that is good for them, but it does not help me. You are very unfeeling about losing this city. You claim you loved it, but you treat the loss like it is nothing. You feel nothing?" asked Louis in anguish.

"I've lost nothing," I replied feeling a little complacent. "For me this is a good story. If I write it well and make people cry I win awards and respect and people know who I am. I guess I was bothered a bit when I first saw the city, but not now. I did enjoy St. Pierre. Today there is nothing left to appreciate. It was never my city anyway. I never invested myself in it."

"You make me sad." He even sounded sorrowful. Louis turned his body to swing his legs around behind me so he could ease into the bed of the wagon." I need to rest now."

A strange smell was in the air. It was not just the burned man moving around. I sniffed trying to identify the odor. "Louis, do you smell cucumbers?"

"Sweet Jesus! God Help us!" Louis cried out in distress.

I volunteered to stop the mule. "Are you in pain? I'll stop the mule to Help."

"No!" Louis screamed. "Do not stop whatever you do! Look in the road on my side of the wagon beside the mule!"

CHAPTER THREE

I glanced to where Louis pointed his finger. My eyes barely noticed signs of unusual movement in the undergrowth beside the road. Then the yellow-brown ribbon of deadly snake slithering out onto the rough dirt road and sinuously moving up beside the mule riveted me. The diamond shaped head was unmistakably like the tip of a spear. The orange eye glowed.

"Louis, that's a fer-de-lance! That is the largest one I've ever seen. He must be seven feet long. What should I do? Should I stop the mule?" I bellowed in panic.

"No. For sure do not stop the mule. Let it plod on. Us natives say to keep talking and ignore the snake. The snake will not bite. So if we do not surprise the snake, if we talk and act like everything is fine, if we do not see the snake, then he does not see us. We just go on our way no bother to anyone."

"Louis, I can't believe you are acting so calm and that is the most God-awful superstition I have ever heard!" I glanced at the white robed man sitting beside me. Louis appeared to be serious. "Do the natives also say if you see your house is on fire and ignore it you won't burn?"

"No, Edward, that would be foolish. So you are from a big city in America. How do you know about our special snake?"

Visibly shaken but trying to appear brave I replied, "I know enough. I know we can't outrun it and we can't kill it. We don't have a machete or a gun. The good Father gave us rosaries for protection. And your voodoo priestess gave you a charm. With the gifts from the two of them, we can strangle the snake. But I don't know how to strangle a snake. Do you? I would say we are at the mercy of the fer-de-lance. What do you say?" I asked cynically.

"So I would say you are right. We are at the mercy of the snake because Father Mary did not have a gun or a machete to loan us for our trip." Louis was resigned to our predicament.

"I should have known this would happen." I was angry at my own stupidity. "I should have borrowed a weapon from someone in Morne Rouge before taking this feeble mule on the road."

"So, I think it is good that we have the feeble old mule. It cannot see the snake because it is nearly blind. And it cannot smell the snake because it can barely breathe. We should appreciate how good the mule is for us."

I glanced at Louis, who was wiping sweat from his brow. It must be fear for him too because the warm air was pleasant and sweet. Now that we were well away from the ash, the aroma of wild orchids filled the air. The sun was mild. I refused to wear my pith helmet, packed in the back of the wagon. Louis did not have a choice about his headgear. He had to wear a straw hat. The sun could hurt his still raw burns.

Louis apparently decided to console me. "So Edward, there was no one in Morne Rouge with a machete or a gun. The only people there are old or very sick and they could not run from the volcano, except for Father Mary, and he must be crazy to stay. So I say keep talking, because there is nothing else to do."

"Okay, I'll talk only because you are right. There is nothing else we can do, but I don't believe your silly superstition." I took another deep breath. The mule plodded along oblivious to its danger. "You know, Louis, this island is incredibly beautiful, and I admire it, but it also has some of the vilest, lowest forms of insects and serpents I have ever seen."

"So what do we have that is so awful? I do not know what other places have, so I do not know what makes us special. So tell me please, Edward."

"Two, beside the snake come to mind. You have ants called fourmi-fou. In my country ants are little black insects. Sometimes they're red. They can sting, but they are more a nuisance than anything. Yours are speckled yellow insects with bites that sting like a fiery needle penetrating the skin.

"In my country we have centipedes that curl up into little puffs of black. But on this island, your centipedes are a foot long and their mouths can bite through leather. You can't kill them because they roll into a protective cocoon."

"So do you see Edward," Louis interrupted, "I am right. We have no trouble with the snake we are ignoring. So keep talking. It is easy for you. My voice still hurts."

"You are right about the snake so far, Louis. The snake is just sliding along ignoring us. I will believe your idea when we get to

Fort-de-France safely. Though it seems to me the condition of the mule is so bad that even if the snake doesn't bite it, it may die anyway and we still have a problem getting to the city. But I will keep talking in hope that you are right and I can believe you.

"I guess it should make me happy the mule is old and plodding. If it could see and smell like a young mule our rickety wagon would be smashed putting us on the ground and the snake would bite us instead of the mule." We grinned at each other. What was I saying? I was unhappy at the prospect of a dead mule whether by accident or design. Louis smiled.

"This is menacing. We can be killed. How can we smile?"

"The clairin for me," came the prompt answer. "Edward, I think you should have drunk some. So too late now. Please to keep talking." Louis smiled again. I turned my face away from the now offending smile and started talking.

"In my country we have a snake that will poison a man with its bite, but it is a gentle snake, it has a warning rattle. Martinique's version doesn't have a rattle. I know you have eight kinds of fer-de-lance here. The most common one is dark gray and speckled with black. It likes to hide in boots. There is a clear bright yellow one that hides among bananas."

"Edward, I hear sighs with your gulps of air as you talk. Let me tell you. We are not so superstitious here as you think. We know where we live and we know the land and how it takes care of us. We know the animals we live with.

"Maybe Father Mary would like to think of our talking as a prayer. Remember what you said, we have no machete, no gun. My throat is burned, my lungs are burned. So Edward, you still talk more. You talk and save us."

"I don't have much else to do I guess, and you say you can't carry on a long conversation, though you've been doing okay so far. I don't know what to say."

"Talk about the snake," urged Louis.

"I can do that at least," I sighed. "This particular fer-de-lance, that might take a bite of our mule, is yellow with big brown triangles on top and a pink underbelly and he is stretching out at least six feet, maybe seven, all beside our mule. You know I think this one is unusually large." I glanced at Louis who was nodding his head in agreement.

"In any case" I continued, "he is fast and deadly. I saw one bite a native once while I was on a visit here. The poor man's flesh chilled. You could see it turn blue, like skin does when you have been in cold air too long."

"Here, only the ocean water turns a person blue, not the air. Is this the same blue, Edward?" asked Louis.

"Yes."

"Please to go on."

"His skin became soft and swollen. It looked puffy like a marshmallow."

"Edward, what is a marshmallow?"

"It's a candy shaped like a cube, like dice. It has white, powdered sugar on the outside and it's squishy inside—mushy. Like a sponge, only you eat it."

"Is it good?"

"Many people like them. I don't. Anyway the man had spots on his skin. You could tell by his screams how dreadful his pain was.

People knew he was going to die and they were talking about shooting him to put him out of agony. Some thought shooting him was a good idea, but others said it was the same as murder. The people kept talking, while the poor man begged for relief. Finally he died by himself and this death was the mercy that ended his pain. No person helped him. My God, Louis, I don't like this snake. This situation makes me uneasy."

"Do not get so shaky, Edward. Would you have killed the man?"

"It wasn't my problem. I was just watching. I know that shooting is the surest way to kill the snake. We can't do that. No gun. I should have known from my newspaper reading in Fort-de-France that the island is totally disrupted with everything thrown out of order, chaotic. Louis, this isn't going to work. I can't keep talking and watching that snake glide along beside the mule. I don't know enough about snakes. I need to do something."

Louis laughed. "So you are doing something. You are talking to me, ignoring the snake, and it works so far. Please to keep talking."

After a great sigh, I continued with renewed determination. "This was supposed to be a simple day trip for us to go from Morne Rouge to Fort-de-France. It's a beautiful day. The palm trees are swaying

gently in the soft sweet breeze. God's in his heaven and all should be

right with the world. How is this happening? Louis, will the snake get

tired and just leave?"

"That is what I hope for. Isn't that what you hope for too?" Louis

asked innocently.

"I don't know. I don't know anything at all about how these

snakes live. You have no idea if the snake will bite the mule or leave

it alone?"

"I do not know what the snake is thinking of any more than you

do."

"Do they bite, just to bite, or only to eat? And does it eat from

hunger or from habit? I wish I knew more about these snakes." I was

starting to feel numb from the stress. This was a deadly snake. I might

be killed right here and no one would ever know what happened to me

because I would rot quickly in the tropical heat.

"Edward, I do not believe what I hear you say because you are a

very smart man who can read and write. The snake kills when it is hungry or if it is afraid because someone or something scared it. I do not know how it could eat a whole mule.

"A mule is a large animal and a snake does not have teeth to take little bites. Since the mule does not scare the snake, the snake should not bite the mule. This mule is moving along steady and slow. If you stop the mule, that might scare the snake. So this snake found the mule and wants to follow beside it and keep it company. This mule did not scare the snake from out of the grass so I think we will be fine. Please to keep talking. I need rest now for sure," Louis finished with a gulp trying to swallow to soothe his dry throat.

I held the reins loosely in my hands and let the mule plod on. I tried to keep my eyes off the snake, but the undulating motion and my fear kept drawing my attention hypnotically.

"Louis, I will try to keep talking but I find it difficult because I still don't believe your idea about the snake ignoring us if we ignore it. Maybe I should sing."

"No, singing is something different from talking and it might scare the snake so just talk," whispered Louis.

"It is very funny to have you tell me talk. It is my job to get other people to talk. That's my job; to get other people to say things I can quote. I don't just talk. I need something to talk about."

"So tell me how you came to my island and why."

"What do you mean, how?"

"Where you leave from? Why? What boat? Where did you land? You know, how you came."

"My boss from the newspaper in Boston sent me. I'm representing the paper and the Associated Press."

"So what is Associated Press?" I could tell that even the whispers were hurting him, but his fear was great too and gave him motivation.

"It is an organization that gathers information and sends it back to a main point for distribution to other newspapers all over the world. I'm sure you've read AP reports in your newspaper."

"No, Edward, I do not read very well. People read to me. Please to go on."

"I was given a pass to sail on the *Dixie*. The *Dixie* was back in port from a training cruise after being made a man-o-war, a military ship. President Roosevelt pulled her out of the Brooklyn Navy Yard

37

to carry cargo and passengers here. I was chosen to be one of forty-three passengers—scientists, physicians, and newsmen like myself. We were quite a mix.

"I left from New York City May 14 and landed in Fort-de-France early in the morning a week later. The day before we landed Mont Pelee had erupted again and there was a fresh eruption on the island of St. Vincent. We learned about these new eruptions on our arrival. The ship went on to the newest eruption and I sent my associate on to the other island.

"We didn't know before landing that Pelee had gone up again, but that explained the fresh smoke and ashes when the ship passed that part of the island. My feature stories focus on the destruction of St. Pierre. I was sent because I knew the city well. There was no point for me going on to St. Vincent.

"The trip wasn't unpleasant, except for the smell of dried cod when the wind blew the wrong direction. Some of the passengers gave lectures, talks about special things they knew. The newspapermen, like myself, put out a small paper and there was a monkey on board named General Wyler, who kept us amused. An empty glove scared him into chattering wildly and trying to find a place to hide. But, a bottle of beer calmed him right down."

"Beer calms many frights," offered Louis. We laughed and thinking the sound might have affected the snake, we both glanced anxiously in that direction. Louis noticed my glance. "Edward, I think you need beer right now. You trouble yourself too much for a foolish reason. There is nothing you can do, so please to go on now. You landed in Fort-de-France?"

"In Fort-de-France I stopped one of the women on the street and asked if she lived there. Her head was wrapped with a scarlet turban and her body was draped with vivid blue and green cloth. Your native women certainly dress colorfully.

"She looked at me and knew I was a stranger. My clothes are too heavy for this climate. It seems I amused her. She answered me with a laugh and a smile. 'Yes, I do live here,' she said. Then she pointed to some other women across the square and said, 'they came from the countryside. They are fleeing the devil. The devil that is breathing fumes from hell through the openings on Mont Pelee."

Louis drew in a quick breath. "The devil breaths again," he whimpered. "So dangerous with bad air. Sparks are better because sparks are from God's blacksmith working at his forge. Please to keep talking." I shook my head with the sad realization that Louis was indeed a typical superstitious native.

"The woman pointed at groups of women walking along the edge of the square. I liked the rhythmic movement of her hand and the sound of her voice. I treasure the quality of the island voices and movements. Do you appreciate the island women, Louis?"

"What do you mean, treasure? You confuse me. Gold is not what you talk about is it?"

"Treasure as something valuable. You islanders speak so smoothly and your voices are so clear it's like a kind of music. Hearing this is always a pleasure for me, something that I treasure."

"Even if we speak poor. Like me?"

"Yes. Even you have this special sound when you speak."

"Please to go on, Edward."

"I tried to determine, that is figure out, her marital status, whether she was single, married, engaged or free, from the way she tied her turban. I forgot what the differences are. Do you know?"

"That is true only for old women and you should not care about them, only the young ones. Please to go on, Edward."

"The women she pointed out to me were carrying baskets, like the women on this island do. But the baskets they were carrying weren't full of things they were going to sell; they were full of everything they owned. They wore pictures of the Virgin Mary over their hearts. To protect them, I guess.

"Louis, do you admire these women who carry such heavy loads and walk so gracefully? Do you notice them? Appreciate them?"

"Of course I do," Louis laughed. "Do you think I am so crazy I do not notice? What man could not notice?"

"I've seen the women with very heavy baskets on their heads. I've been told they carry up to eighty pounds. That's incredible. You know I've never seen one of the men do that."

"Men do not do women's work. So please to go on."

"I enjoyed seeing the marble statue of Napoleon's Josephine in the Place d'Armes again. With the sandbox trees lining the park and the broad promenade all around, it is very scenic. Then with the sea on two sides of the square and the bay full of ships before it, it is a quite remarkable port."

"So we don't like Josephine very much," Louis grumbled. "She was born here, but she did not help the people here. Please to go on, Edward. We must keep talking."

"It was exciting for me to come back here, even with this morbid assignment. Walking the streets was stimulating. Such movement. So many people. The streets are so narrow that all the extra people crowded in made it difficult to walk without being jostled about.

"I wanted to submerge myself in the spirit of the city. My plan was to use it to contrast with whatever I found in St. Pierre. I wanted to absorb everything. Louis, have you ever noticed how the island smells?"

Louis answered, "Sometimes, but mostly if the smell is bad. Like garlic. What do you notice?"

"The air is always warm and fragrant. There is always a breeze that brings the scent of blooming flowers, so mixed up that no single smell dominates. The air is like a bouquet all around.

"And I prize the noises of the marketplace. You hear the vendors trying to attract buyers because they have the finest mangoes, or alligator pears that cut so beautifully, like soft green cheese. Your fishmongers have the freshest fish. The pastry seller has the most flavorful and delicate pastry. Even the red clay cooking pots, are artistically stacked."

I paused in my musing and stared at the snake. "Louis, look. Do you think the snake is moving differently?" My voice was strained. "I believe the snake is changing the way it moves. What is going to happen to us?"

CHAPTER FOUR

My body was radiating pain. From my cold toes to the top of my aching head, all my physical being was distressed. I was bruised and sore and felt I'd been severely beaten. What happened? I didn't know.

I cautiously tried to move my head. Slowly, it responded. I found my reluctant body moved on command, but it disputed the idea. What else could I move? I flexed my hands. They worked, slowly and awkwardly, but they worked. Then I tried to open my eyes in spite of the pain surrounding my head, and radiating all directions. That pain spread out enveloping me. I could not see anything clearly through my clouded vision. What happened? Where was I?

I felt pressure in my chest. Anxiety started in my pounding heart and tried to move up and out of my body. I counseled myself to be calm. I was alive and I had time to find out what was going on. Death was not near. There was no reason to panic. *Be calm*, I thought over and over.

I tried to get a sense of where I was, even though I couldn't see. I knew I must concentrate. I must be logical about my condition. *Be calm* I told myself. I forced myself to breathe deeply and slowly, until

the feeling of panic diminished. I talked to myself, repeating over and

over, *I'm calm and I'm sane enough to know there is nothing I can do*

for myself right now.

I sensed I was not outside. There was no movement of air, no

temperature changes, but I couldn't tell just where I was. Inside, but

where? I thought there might be people around me, but I couldn't see

anything distinctly. The effort of trying to lift my head and open my

eyes exhausted me. I needed more rest. I closed my eyes easily. I

would sleep and think about my predicament later. I didn't have the

energy to ponder my circumstances now.

Someone was trying to lift and hold the side of my head to feed

me some soup, or broth, or something warm. I tried to raise my head

to help, but it made me dizzy. The other person lifted my head for me.

I could not help.

I summoned my energy and laboriously stretched my arm around

to the back of my head where most of the pain was coming from. I

felt a large sensitive lump under my matted hair. I gave up trying to

explore my injury and let my hand fall back to my side. No wonder I felt so sore. I must have taken quite a beating to have a bump like that on my head.

I opened my eyes slowly. I could not tell, but it appeared there were two Negro women trying to feed me. I closed my eyes briefly, then opened them and looked one more time. I closed one eye and saw it was a single woman. When I opened the other eye, I saw two of them again. Drinking the broth exhausted me and I closed my eyes as the woman gently laid me down.

I did not know how much time had passed when I awoke. There was activity around me. I thought perhaps a meal was in preparation. The smells had somehow changed. I opened one eye. Then the other. My vision blurred. I closed one eye. The blur disappeared. What was going on? Where was I? After a moment I decided to try both eyes again.

I opened my eyes and tried to sit up. I was unsuccessful. I had the sense of people around me, but I couldn't see anyone through the heavy fog. I needed rest. I dropped back into oblivion.

I felt someone trying to help me change positions. I slowly opened my eyes. My vision was still blurry. I thought I could see shapes of people in a shelter. The space felt enclosed. Though it was very dark, my perception was of being in a room. *Could it be a cave?* The noises were strange, unfamiliar. *What kind of room was this?* I concentrated and the twin Negro women appeared before me once more. They were mumbling something to me I couldn't understand. It was not unpleasant. It sounded agreeable. It was not threatening, but it was incomprehensible.

Someone helped me sit up. After I sat up, she blocked the light entering one eye with a dark blue scarf. She tied the cloth over my eye and around the back of my head. This eliminated my double vision. There was only one woman when I used only one eye and I felt suddenly reassured. This must be a hospital and the women were nurses taking care of me. I looked around slowly. I was inside. It was a small room.

Several people were doing something, moving about and using their hands. A Negro man came into focus. I knew there were no male nurses. There was something frightening about this man. I knew instinctively this man was dangerous. I realized with alarm that all the people I could see were Negro!

My position was more alarming than I had first supposed. What had happened to me? I looked down at my own white skin. I did not belong here. I knew better than to go into a crowd of Negroes alone. Where was I?

How has this happened? What danger am I in? A group of Negro agitators murdered more than one solitary white man without explanation. It was not safe for a single white person in such a group. Why am I here? Where am I? I am afraid. What is going to happen to me?"

The man came toward me holding out a cup of steaming liquid for me to drink. I wanted no part of this man. I knew this man was dangerous. I knew this man wanted to kill me. The drink was poison. I mustered all my strength and knocked the mug out of the man's hands. The man looked startled and turned to the women saying something.

One of the woman kept babbling her gibberish as she approached me. She kept repeating one word over and over. "Edward," she was calling to me, but I did not understand what she was saying. I only wanted to sleep. The woman kept repeating something over and over, so I tried to concentrate on her words. I still could not tell what she was saying.

I carefully tried to lie down and the woman helped me once she understood what I wanted. Exhausted I lay back on the bed and closed my eyes tightly to keep the danger away. I slipped into a deep, dark, comforting sleep, without drinking anything.

"Edward." I heard someone calling. I opened my eyes to see the black man with a cup of something hot in my hand. "Edward," the man repeated. It was pleasing to hear something as familiar as my name, *but how did this man know it*? Then the man started to speak the same gibberish the other people in the room were using to communicate. Why couldn't I understand this language?

I shook my head and tried to push the liquid away with my hand. I did not want anything this man was going to give me. I knew couldn't trust this stranger. They were drugging me. They were holding me for ransom. I drew back from the man with the cup.

The woman who had been taking care of me saw my refusal to drink. She took the cup away from the man and moved it slowly until I could smell it. It smelled good. The woman had been feeding me and everything she gave me was beneficial. It must be safe. With the woman's help, I drank the broth and lay back exhausted. I was ready for more sleep.

It was quiet in the room. I heard birds singing outside and wind in the trees. These were unfamiliar bird songs. I recognized the cock-a-doodle-doo of a rooster, but the other birds sounded more exotic, foreign or alien somehow. Some of them were shrill. I did not know of any screeching birds like this in Boston.

The wind didn't sound right either. I was certain that the sound I heard was decidedly wind in the trees, but it was softer than what I was familiar with. *The leaves did not rustle like Fall leaves. It didn't sound like a tree with leaves at all. What other trees were there?*

I heard someone in the room moving and opened my eyes. The scarf around my head was gone. For the first time, my eyes focused clearly. I saw a Negro woman starting to warm something on a wood burning stove. I could see—and what I saw still did not make sense to me.

I was in a small room. There was a table with a kerosene lamp on it. A picture of the Virgin Mary was by the door. There were two narrow plank beds in the room. I was sleeping in one of them. The man who had called me Edward was sleeping in the other bed. Both beds had crucifixes hanging over them. There were three other people sleeping in the room on mats on the dirt floor. The curved shapes of the light covers suggested the sleeping figures were female.

I felt the back of my head. The bump was still there, but I felt less pain than before. Then I noticed the Negro man appeared taller than I was by more than a few inches. He looked malnourished. There was something wrong with the man's skin. Anxiety seized me. *They kept me alive for something. What was it?*

The man from the other bed looked at me with a smile. He walked to the woman saying something in their language. The man nodded at me. I sat up on one elbow, with considerable discomfort, to look at them.

The woman put something in a cup and walked toward me. She smiled at me and said something I could not understand. I tried to sit fully upright to take the drink she offered me, but I was too weak. The man came over and helped prop me up, then he walked away and went through a door at the far end of the room. I saw this door led outside.

I eagerly drank the beverage a woman handed me. I felt hungry. I liked the broth, but I hoped they would give me some solid food soon. I thought the drink was a spicy beef broth, but I didn't recognize exactly what it was. In any case it was tasty and I enjoyed it.

The woman went to the window and opened the shutters. There was no glass in the windows. Light flooded the little room. I could plainly see into all corners. I now knew I was in a small native hut of some kind. *But where? Why?* I knew I could figure out my condition if I could only concentrate.

I studied the tree outside the window. It was not a maple tree. It was not a palm tree. The leaf wasn't frilly. I had seen some palm trees with a solid leaf like this tree had; but I was sure it wasn't a palm tree. This tree had a long full leaf. Where had I seen this tree before?

I studied the tree, searching its branches with my eyes. There was something growing in the tree. It was a group of shoots, finger-like spikes, growing upward. It was a banana tree! I was in a tropical climate. I began to feel positive about my situation. I had an idea of where I was. I was on an island somewhere in the Caribbean.

The sleeping women began to stir. The day was about to begin. Maybe I could learn more about my circumstances. The man came back into the single room house and I knew I had seen this person somewhere before. I knew I should be afraid.

The man was wearing shorts. He had a wide-brimmed hat in his hands. No shoes. Nothing else. I could see scars over much of the man's body. Healing patches of pink skin on my arms, chest and legs, were in puzzling contrast to his untouched face.

"Edward." The man started to talk to me, but I could not understand any more than my name. I drew away from the man. The man stopped talking to me and said something to the women.

The man went to a jug and poured some water into a cup. He brought the cup to me and said strange words over it, *tasse, eau*. The man went around the room pointing at objects and giving them names. He picked up some pieces of cloth and said a word, *drap*.

Something clicked in my memory. The man was speaking French. Could I remember French? I knew I had spoken it once. At least I knew what the language was now, though any command of it escaped me for the moment.

This was tiring. I could not participate for long. I soon felt exhausted. I slipped back into sleep.

I woke up to drink the broth an older plump Negress brought. Then, without warning, the woman pulled my blanket back and began washing me and rubbing lotion on me. This was quite pleasurable, but also embarrassing. I was naked, but she had gray hair and I was too weak and discouraged to try for modesty. In any case I was too powerless to protest. When she finished the front of me, she helped me lie on my back and proceeded to wash and apply the lotion to the rest of my body. She turned me over and ended by massaging my back. It felt sublime.

I relaxed and began to drift into an agreeable sleep when she turned me over and started rolling my head around with her hands. She moved my head in a circle, to the side, then back, to the other side and forward. I grew dizzy. She stopped and I considered the consequences of throwing up.

Her next move was to seize my right arm. She lifted it and bent it at the elbow several times. She moved to the left arm and repeated the same action. She reached for my leg, bent it at the knee and moved the toes and ankle up and down repeatedly. She repeated this on the other side. She went back to my right hand and moved the fingers and wrist up and down. She pulled this hand across my body. She repeated the same motions with the left hand.

What she was doing perplexed me, but it felt good, so I wasn't going to stop her. She finished and covered me with a light blanket. I drifted into the comforting darkness of sleep.

When the women woke me up to eat, I knew I had survived the effects of whatever had befallen me. I recognized the people were speaking French mixed with a native patois. I could communicate with them and find out what was going on.

I faced my first solid food gratefully. During this evening meal of chicken and sweet potatoes, I sat up to eat and spoke in the French I finally grasped. I said, "I am feeling better. I want to thank you for your help. Have I been in an accident? Where am I? What are you going to do with me?"

"I will tell you tomorrow," said the tall black man. "Do you remember me?" he asked.

"I know I have seen you, but I do not remember your name," I responded.

"Perhaps you will remember after a good nights sleep."

One of the women thrust a warm mug of something dark and murky into my hands. I drank the liquid without much thought. Everything they gave me to drink was pleasant in taste and aroma and this drink was no different. *Or was it?* I felt unusual warmth creeping over me and I lay down to sleep again. My sleep was deep and the last thing I thought about was the identity of the black man and why he was dangerous.

CHAPTER FIVE

The noisy creaking of the opening door roused me from sleep. I felt a sense of alarm. Through the open door I caught a reassuring glimpse of a sun-washed day that calmed me. *Had an entire night passed? Or a whole day? How long had I been here?* I moved my battered body slowly.

When the large, old Negress saw my movement, she opened the shutters to the beautiful daylight. Though bruised and tender, I felt at least among the living again. Looking outside I saw Louis Ciparis arguing with a young man. He was obviously angry. The shouts were loud and hands were thrashing about. It was not apparent what the disagreement was about. Suddenly Louis threw something into the trees and slapped the other man, who went running off the opposite direction from whatever it was that Louis threw away.

I tried to remember what I knew about this man. I never saw anything but an even temper in Louis, who seemed generally friendly and easygoing. As Louis entered the shack seeming completely calm and at ease, I remembered why I was afraid. Louis was a murderer.

The sudden chill I felt did not leave me easily. I knew I must talk to Louis to find out what was going on. There was no other way.

I tried to appear calm and not show the anxiety I felt. "Louis, what happened to me?" I asked. "What kind of accident did we have and who are these people?"

"So you know me now. That is good. Yesterday you did not remember much beside your name and a few simple words. So you even acted afraid of me. You would not take the broth I offered you. So this is a good sign. I will have to tell Marie." Louis started to turn to leave.

"Please, please, don't go," I implored. "Tell me what happened first."

"So you do not remember?"

"No."

"What is the last thing you do remember?" probed Louis.

"I remember a fer-de-lance on the side of the road next to the mule. You were in the wagon bed resting. I was driving the mule. That is all I can remember."

Louis sat on the edge of the bed opposite me. He said, slowly and with great thought, "So I did not see anything happen, because I was in the wagon bed. The snake must have bit the mule, or it could be the mule died then the snake bit it after it was dead. But the mule would have taken a little time to die and fall after the snake bit it. So no one knows for sure what way it happened, anyhow the mule fell dead and the wagon tipped over. Fang marks were on the mule, but maybe the fall of the mule made the snake upset and so he bit the mule. So do you see what I mean no one knows for sure?

"So the falling wagon shook me awake. I thought I could protect myself from great injury with all the blankets that were surrounding me. But then the blankets pulled tight around me and the pain was terrible. Instead of protecting me, the blankets hurt me. So I was all tangled up with blankets and it took some long time for the people who found us to get me out of the wagon.

"So I saw where the wagon landed in a small ditch along the side of the road and I saw the dead mule. I did not see the snake. I think he left when the people came to save us. Some had the machete to kill a snake but no one told me the snake died.

"So when I saw you, you were in a heap on your back at the base of a tree. Marie, the healing person, said you hit your head and would be asleep for a while. She gave me something to stop the pain then they brought us both here to take care of us."

"These people intend to take care of me then let me go?" I questioned disbelieving. "No ransom? Nothing? Just get me well and let me go?"

"These people are caring for both of us," answered Louis. "But of course. They are good people. So we are lucky they found us quickly after the accident. Maybe that was my pacquet at work. The Voodoienne warned me it was a dangerous trip. So now I know what she meant."

"Who are these people?" I asked.

"They work on the plantation we were passing, before the snake bit the mule or the mule died and the snake bit it after. Whatever. The cart made a little noise, or maybe a big noise when it fell over. I do not know. I only heard myself scream since I so much hurt again.

"So one person found us. Maybe he heard my scream or the wagon crash. My scream is maybe not so loud because I did not want to hurt my throat. I do not know how, but he found us then he got others to help."

"How long was I unconscious?"

"At least one week," replied Louis. "So then it took you another week? Sometimes awake. Sometimes asleep. Now you are awake and can talk, and it has been about two weeks or perhaps a little more."

"I don't remember anything but the snake along the edge of the road," I mused.

"The woman, Marie, tells me you will never remember some things. She says you must stay in bed another week, or maybe five days. So they will exercise your body and you will be able to walk when you get up. But we can stay here until we are both well. At least well enough to travel pleasantly."

"Where are we?" I asked, still bewildered.

"It has no special name here. So it is part of a plantation about halfway between Morne Rouge and Fort-de-France. We will be able to get a ride with the food going to market. Or, we can walk, when the time comes."

"How is it possible your burns are healed?" I wondered out loud. It was amazing. "When I first saw you there was blood oozing from raw open places on your back and you had very little flesh at all. If it has only been two weeks, how have your burns healed so quickly?"

"Edward," said Louis, shaking his head, "I do not know. Marie practices good voodoo and has magic lotions and things to drink that heal. So when you get up in a week, we will have a special healing ritual for both of us. She says that will help even more. So she does not want you to go to white doctors. She is afraid they will not do the right things to heal you. So, Edward, we will be fine. But tell me, why are you afraid of me?"

I was stunned. I did not feel my fear was obvious. Mustering all of my strength I snapped, "I'm not afraid of you, Louis."

"Then why do you push away the broth when I try to give you some? You even knocked it from my hand. But you drink it when the women give it to you? You draw back when I come near you in the room and you are not all awake. Why do you pull away from me when I come near you? So think for a minute and give me an honest answer. Do not make me angry. So I do not want to be played with. I want you to be honest with me. So why are you afraid of me?"

I sat quietly, considering my position. I knew that Louis couldn't possibly know what I was thinking. Louis was now stronger than I was. He was up and walking and slapping other people around, and Louis was a larger man. If we came to blows and I won, very unlikely, I would have no idea where to go or if anyone would help me. The other people here might also be afraid of Louis. I still wanted to know just what crime Louis had committed. I would also like to know how Louis' burns healed so quickly, an even bigger feather in my cap to write about. I had to stay put and take my chances. There was no place to run.

I answered truthfully. "I don't want to make you angry. I will be honest with you. There are two reasons. First, I read about the unrest on the island where white men were killed with no witnesses. Second, I was told you are a murderer."

Louis burst out laughing. "So I am a murderer. I will bet that you do not know how many I have murdered or why. This is very funny!"

Louis was obviously amused. I didn't see anything funny in the situation.

Finally Louis grew serious and looked steadily at me with a growing frown. "So who told you?" he asked with a stern voice.

"Two different people. The first was a housekeeper for Father Mary. She came into my room with fresh towels early one morning and said something. I was just waking up and didn't hear her plainly but I thought it was a warning. I asked her to repeat what she said. She said that the man, Ciparis, was evil. A murderer who killed white men.

"Then I met the men who found you. They said they only heard a rumor, that you killed a white soldier in a fight over politics. They did know they found you in a solitary confinement cell and that minor criminals don't go to those cells."

"I will not discuss my crime with you now," said Louis sharply. "I must have more information. So tell me about this unrest you read about. I was in prison and I do not know of any special problem."

I began uneasily. "I learned about the unrest on the island from newspaper articles. I got the newspapers from the editor of *Les*

Colonies when I arrived on the island. I wanted to know everything reported before and after the eruption. There was an election coming up and the situation was very tense."

"Yes, yes. So that I know. This is nothing new." Louis provided his own explanation. "The Progressive Party, the white man's party, always wants to win and they pay people to vote for them. They did not want the Radical Party to win because Amedee Knight is so good for us. With him we get total control of how to run the island. So this is nothing new. This unrest has been here before."

"What is new, Louis, is that the Progressive Party candidate admitted there was a need for reform. This caused the people to protest. They were angry."

"The white people or the black people?"

"Both."

"Please to go on, Edward."

"With the people of St. Pierre all upset about the election, and the volcano making noises, the governor thought white people would leave the city. He sent soldiers to be sure no one left. One of the soldiers was killed and another disappeared. The newspaper reported that natives did it."

Louis exploded, "So when any white man disappears, or is found dead, the natives are blamed, but we may not do this work. White men kill other white men and hide the bodies away in places there white people don't go alone. So we are blamed and no one is arrested. So tell me, did they arrest anyone?

"No. At least I didn't read that anyone was arrested."

The men paused in thought then Louis said, "So the election is over, do you know who won?"

"No, I didn't pay any attention. It wasn't important for what I was doing."

"So then, Edward, the election is over and the soldiers are gone. Also the city is gone. So you have nothing to fear because everything is over."

"Louis, you haven't told me about your crime. I may still have something to fear." I decided to be daring. "Are you a murderer?" I asked Louis.

Louis answered quietly and deliberately, "Sometime, perhaps I will tell you, but it is not important for me to tell you now. It is only important for you. So before I tell you anything you want to know, I must hear everything you know about the disaster. I must learn all about the dreadful death that came down on my people. You must tell me what I need to know. That you tell me is a necessary answer about living and dying for you if you want to know about me. So do you understand me, Edward? You must tell me everything you know." The quiet-spoken Louis growled out the last few words.

I nodded that I understood. I understood that I had to tell Louis everything I knew because there was some important information about the eruption I had that Louis needed. This was a matter of life and death. I had the feeling it was *my* life and death Louis was talking about. If Louis didn't learn what he wanted to know, I wouldn't live to write anything further. I also knew I had no idea about what it was that Louis wanted to find out.

"So I can tell you that you do not need to fear me if you tell me honestly what I want to know. Besides you think it is important to your work to know my story so that is another reason to tell me. You are an educated man. You can tell me very easily." Louis turned away and started to leave. "I am going to find the woman, Marie, now."

"Who is Marie?" I asked.

"So you will meet her. She is our powerful healer. She has taken care of you herself. She told the others what to do when she wasn't here." Louis started to go to the door.

I stopped him. "Before you go, are my writing materials still around, or did everything get lost when the cart overturned?"

"Everything from the cart is near, Edward. So what do you want?" asked Louis.

"Paper and my pen. I want to make some notes. You said I have to stay in bed another week. Are you sure someone can't take me to Fort-de-France?"

"No, for good reasons. You must tell me what you know about the eruption and Marie wants us both to stay here so she can take care of us. So they have sent word to Father Mary, and that is enough. Marie fears we will not heal as well as we can if we go to the ordinary doctors. Do you understand me?"

"Yes, I understand. I am a prisoner here, but you say no harm will come to me as long as I tell you about the eruption."

"No, Edward. Not a prisoner. A guest with these people and no harm will come to you if you are honest with me. So I will go and get your pen and paper."

I slumped back into the bed exhausted from the effort of sitting up and talking. I was overwhelmed to realize I ever thought of fighting with Louis. There was no way I was strong enough. I wanted the comfort of sleep but it wouldn't come because I was still upset by the confrontation.

Now I understood what happened. Louis himself was never in a coma and he told the others to keep me alive because he had to learn something I knew. Louis said this was a matter of life or death.

What a perplexing situation I was caught in. Because of this accident, I was now in the custody of a group of Negroes who, for some reason, did not want to take me to white men, of my own kind, for medical treatment. First, Louis was in my care. Now I was dependent on Louis.

From a mist of troubled listlessness, I heard the soft clear musical voice of a Martinican woman. I did not want to face a threat to my life again. I wanted to hold the safety my stupor provided. The voices continued, forcing me to part with my comforting private world.

"Edward, Marie is here to meet you." Louis called me out of my lethargy, shaking me.

I saw a beautiful woman standing beside Louis. Marie was more than beautiful. She was magnificent. Breathtaking. She was a warm, nut-brown color, not the ebony of Louis. Her long dark hair flowed into the curves of her body. The draping of the long dress she wore hid nothing. She was an example of the admirable blending of culture and race that set the island of Martinique apart.

"So, Edward, tell Marie if you recognize me," directed Louis.

"Yes, I recognize you," I answered quietly and carefully. "You are Louis Ciparis, the survivor of the eruption of Mont Pelee."

"This is useful. I hear you speak and know you are back with us," comforted Marie. "You gave us a scare. We thought we might lose you and we did not want a dead white man to bury." Her voice entranced me as much as her appearance.

"We sent word to Father Mary about the accident," said Louis. "When we are able, we will walk to the plantation and they will give us a ride to Fort-de-France. The people at the plantation house do not know we are here. Only Father Mary knows. Marie wanted to save you herself. She feared they could not help you. Marie has very strong magic." Ciparis nodded toward the young woman standing to his left. "So you see what she has done for me, and for you also."

"How do I thank you properly for my care?" I asked.

In her musical voice Marie answered, "Get up and walk again. Let everyone see what good work I do. Louis said you wanted this paper and pen." Marie handed me the items. "Do not work too long with them. You need much more rest. I will see you later." She smiled and left the shack.

It felt good to have my pen back in my hand. It was familiar. Something I understood. Where should I start in this strange tale I had to tell? I started to make a list. I would make notes under the different topics as they occurred to me.

Pen in hand I began my list:

Accident

First visit with Louis Ciparis

Louis' amazing recovery from extensive burns

Own injuries

Meeting Marie

I also thought about why I was bothering to make notes. I smiled to myself. It was a good sign. It meant I intended to live and write a good article about the survivor. On these islands, murder was punishable by hanging. What a piece. I could see it in print. *Prisoner watches his own scaffold being built, yet is the only one to live.*

I paused between each entry on my list and my own intruding thoughts. Writing took enormous effort. I didn't know why it was so hard. My hand just did not want to work. I put the paper down, finished for now. I didn't know if what I wrote made any sense. I was tired and besides, I couldn't think anymore.

I reminded myself Marie had ordered another week of bed rest. Maybe she knew what she was doing. Maybe that was exactly what I needed. I chided myself as I felt fatigue overcoming me again.

Louis saw me put the paper down and came to sit on the edge of his own bed opposite mine. "So finished already?"

"Yes, it's making me tired," I replied.

"So do you want to talk?"

"That would be fine with me, Louis. I can't do much else and I must stay in bed. I can't disagree with a beautiful woman, like Marie, who knows what is best for me."

Louis found this remark very amusing and laughed. "She is a beautiful woman. She is a gifted and desirable woman. So it would be very easy to love such a person."

"Louis, you're healed and even your voice has changed."

"How has my voice changed?"

"You sound stronger, more alive. Your voice is richer when you talk, more the quality most natives have. Not all raspy as if you had ash still caught in your throat." I yawned. "I think I shouldn't talk now, just get some more sleep. I will talk to you later, Louis. I'm not going anywhere."

As I drifted off to sleep I heard Louis' voice. "So do not worry. When you can walk there will be a healing ceremony for us to be sure

73

of our recovery. A healing ceremony and other special things. So we will both be fine if you are honest to me. Do not worry."

I wanted to know what a healing ceremony was, but I didn't have the strength to ask.

CHAPTER SIX

The tantalizing smell of coffee and something sweet cooking over a campfire drifted in through the open door welcoming me to another day. The aroma made me hungry for the first time. I hoped I would get some solid food soon. Perhaps tonight at the latest I would get something besides broth. At least now I could ask.

"So you are awake again." Louis greeted me and came over to my bed to help me sit up. "Did you smell the good food?"

"Yes, my mouth is watering. Do I get to eat soon?"

"I don't know. Maybe, if Marie thinks you are ready. She did say that you could have some bread if you asked for it. They are baking some sweet potatoes and I think there is one more than usual, so maybe that means she thinks you are ready to eat. So are you hungry right now?"

"Yes, I'm hungry," came my quick response. "I want to eat something solid now, even if it's only some bread. The liquids I've been given, the broth and such, are good but I want something solid to build my strength."

"So let me get some bread for you. This bread that these women bake is better than anything. You will like it. When we are ready to go they will make a special bread they have for travel." Louis handed me a slice of dark bread and I bit into it gratefully without any hesitation. I was ravenous.

"So while we are waiting for more food, can you tell me why Father Mary let them have the voodoo ceremony for me?" asked Louis. "He does not like voodoo and even though I did not know the man before, I heard he does not like it. Everyone on the island knows he does not like voodoo. He is very against it. So why did he allow it?"

"I only know what he said to me while we were waiting for you. He said he had to give in to corruption one more time and he hated doing it, but the local witch doctor said she could give you a painless journey and he couldn't. Now I know he was talking about clairin, your special rum, to keep you pain free. Still he wanted to show you that it was wrong, so he took me with him to his rooms to get the rosary he gave you. He gave one to me also."

"You saw his room? So what does it look like? I have never seen the room of a priest."

"It was small. About the same size as the room you were in when I first saw you. It had a plain wood bed and a chest of drawers. It looked like a religious museum. I counted eight statues of the Virgin Mary, one Saint Joseph, one Saint John, a crucifix. There were too many crosses and hearts for me to count. He took the rosaries he gave us out of a whole drawer filled with them."

"So what did he say?

"He said voodoo is evil, but forbidding it didn't end the practice. He said you use it behind his back and he isn't supposed to know about it, which makes him very angry. He also said that practicing voodoo is a superstition you use most when you think God is punishing you. He says you go back to the old ways and practice voodoo even more when things are disturbed, like bad weather, or anything you see as a bad omen."

"So how does he look when he says these things?"

"When he talked about voodoo he frowned and seemed to tremble, feeling rage I think and his gray eyes flashed in anger. He decided he would give in a little to make the trip easier for you. If it was easier for you, it was also easier for me. He was trying to help both of us."

"So why did he ask you to bring me to Fort-de-France?"

"He couldn't do it himself. He had sick people to care for. He thought it would be an advantage for me because I could talk to you over a period of time and get a story out of it; besides, I had to go to Fort-de-France anyway. I agreed with him that it was a tremendous opportunity for me." I paused, remembering his reaction the first time I asked him about his crime. Then I forged ahead because my purpose needed to be revealed at some time. I wanted an answer. "My feature stories about the eruption should win some awards for me and interviewing the one survivor, you, could be my ultimate achievement, my best work in this series."

"So how did you come to Morne Rouge?" His reply was calm. He was ignoring my message. Apparently he would answer me in his own good time. But at least now he wasn't spitting fire at me.

"I walked from St. Pierre with Henri Duvall, a scientist I met there while we were both looking at the ruins. It was a hot, unpleasant walk through piles of ash with no shade anywhere. All the trees were gone. Every one of them burned. We left the smell of sulfur in St. Pierre and came to the scent of roses at Morne Rouge, so arriving was a relief. Also, Morne Rouge was cooler. We were very happy to get to Morne Rouge. The difference between the two places is like the difference between heaven and hell." I paused. I was pleased with myself. I liked comparing them as heaven and hell. It was something I might write, but I never spoke like this before. It was not my job to talk.

"So please to go on, Edward. Tell me the whole story including the time you saw me."

I began my report again, with more self-assurance. "The differences between the two places was stunning because behind us was emptiness and ahead of us was life. Nothing looked wrong with the village when you first looked at it, except there was a light sprinkling of volcanic dust in the street.

"I told Henri I didn't hear a sound, not even a dog barking, and I asked him if he was sure there were people in Morne Rouge. He assured me there were people, but not many.

"As Henri spoke, we saw a priest coming toward us at a rapid pace, his hands stretched out in welcome. His cassock fluttered in the breeze and he had a pith helmet on his head. When we met face to face, I saw the cassock and helmet were both shabby and worn.

"Father Mary was cheerful. He appeared to have no cares. His appearance reminded me of a Boston-Irish priest. Louis, do you know what I mean?"

Louis shook his head no. "I do not know Boston-Irish," he answered.

"It describes someone who lives in Boston, the city I come from, who came from the country of Ireland. Mostly a white man with a red complexion. A young face with gray eyes and maybe some gray hair. He is usually very light hearted and friendly."

"I understand. Please to go on, Edward."

"As we shook hands with him he said, 'I'm Father Mary. Welcome to Morne Rouge,' in a strong friendly voice. He told us, 'People saw you walking up the path. I left instructions that my helpers are to meet us with cool drinks on our return. I suggested a refreshing rum drink.'

"We introduced ourselves. Father Mary said he was pleased to meet us in this time of great upheaval and sorrow. He wanted to know why we were there.

"I told Father Mary that Henri told me he heard there was a survivor from St. Pierre at Morne Rouge. I asked if that was true. He said it was and we could meet you. He said he had an asylum for the old, poor and infirm. The 'castoffs left behind' he called them, 'the ones that couldn't get away.'

"Since so many people had left, Father Mary borrowed an empty house and set up a small lazaret, and that is where you were. He said we would visit you after we rested and cooled down, but we mustn't stay too long. It would over tire you."

"So can you tell me exactly what Father Mary said about me?"

"I'm not exactly sure, but he said something like 'It is amazing this one is still alive. God has granted him a blessed gift of life. There must be glorious missions in store for him,' or something close to that."

"Please to go on, Edward. What happened next?"

"There was a light cover of ash on the street, so dust came up over our feet and created little clouds around us as we walked. It looked like a totally abandoned village, a ghost town. Many of the houses were boarded-up. Others stood with doors and windows open.

"Henri asked if Mr. Arnoux was still there. Mr. Arnoux was another scientist he wanted to talk to. Father Mary said he was either in the village or very near.

"I asked Father Mary if he saw the eruption. He said he had. He told us that Mr. Arnoux saw the eruption from Precheur. I thought this was exciting information. I could learn two different views of what the eruption looked like to people who actually saw it.

"Father Mary led us to a pleasant, cool room. The waiting beverages were cold rum drinks as he had requested. It occurs to me now that this is strange given his reaction to your drinking rum before we left. In any case, we talked for a while, about nothing in particular. Father Mary was a good host and made us feel relaxed and welcome. He even asked us some silly riddles."

"So what do you mean, silly riddles?"

"He asked us a question and wanted us to give an answer. One was, do you know when tennis was first played in the Bible? I said tennis was never mentioned in the Bible. He said I was wrong. It was when Moses served in Pharaoh's court and we laughed."

"I do not understand, Edward."

"Tennis is a modern game played with rackets, a ball and a net. The ground where it is played is called a court."

"So I still do not understand, but please to go on. What happened next?"

"We talked some more. Father Mary explained he felt it was his job to stay in Morne Rouge, in spite of any danger from the volcano, because someone had to take care of the poor unfortunate people who could not leave. He felt God would take care of him, so he could stay safely. He did not need to leave.

"He took us to see you and on the way he told us about the two men who found you four days after the disaster. They were from Precheur and went into St. Pierre to salvage anything they could. Even though there was little hope of survivors, they went to search for some, under the rubble and such. They found you by accident. You were crying out from a jail cell. They brought you here because they didn't know what else to do. They didn't think you would survive long enough to get to Father Mary.

"Father Mary didn't know if you would live once he got you settled. He had no physician, no pharmacy, no surgeon, nothing to keep such a badly burned person alive, or even very comfortable. You were too injured to travel to Fort-de-France, even if it had been possible. But Father Mary wanted to send you on as soon as practical, and in the meantime he did his best.

"Father Mary told us when he was ill he dosed himself with quinine, strychnine and iron. It was all he had on hand and it wouldn't do you any good. He had sent to Fort-de-France for linseed oil, limewater, phenic acid and bandages to treat you, but nothing arrived.

"He said he thought you would live. That God was helping you in your fight and had saved you for some grand purpose because you have nothing here to help you. You had no family and a family is what usually helps such a victim. He said God gave you a strong will, or you would not have survived the four days.

"Father Mary opened the door of a wood house on main street and motioned for us to follow him. He went down a short hall and opened the door to the plain, small room you were in. The room was hot and foul. And since it had no windows it was gloomy and smelled like decaying flesh and old blood. Flies were buzzing all around your room. I put a handkerchief to my face and Henri gagged.

"You were sitting naked on a dirty, dark blue striped mattress on a wooden cot. You had a bloody sheet over your head like an Arabian burnoose, with the fabric loosely gathered in around your waist and legs."

"So Edward, I do not want to interrupt you when you are talking so good, but what is this Arabian thing you talk about?"

"It's like a cloak, or cape, with a hood."

"So please to go on now."

"I never saw a man more horribly burned than you were. The first things I noticed when I looked at you were your hands, then your legs and feet. Your hands were covered with yellow stinking matter. All your limbs were dreadfully burned and swollen. Your face had a stern look but it was free of burns, totally untouched and your hair was not scorched or singed. Your eyebrows were normal too, but the burns on your body were so deep that blood oozed from them. It didn't look like you had much skin left on your legs or arms. At least half your body was burned."

Louis shifted uncomfortably on his bed. "I did look very bad and I did smell very bad and that is why the other man threw up."

"Yes. He said he had expected something different, cleaner. Even though Father Mary warned us he had nothing to treat you with, he still expected something that smelled like medicine or a hospital. And this was two weeks after the men found you. What we couldn't understand was why your back was so badly burned, yet your shirt and chest were untouched. Father Mary had the women wash your shirt and it was folded on the table beside your bed. It looked like a fresh shirt."

"Edward, I do not understand this myself. It must be something like when a child spills something hot on his body and it goes inside of his clothes and it burns him, but the clothes are still whole. Sometime I will tell you what it was like in the cell, but for now I want you to talk to me, to tell me everything you know. So please to go on."

"Father Mary removed the sheet to check you. You were sitting up, but you didn't have the strength to sit upright so you slouched, all silent, not moving. I thought the only other position would be for you to lie on your stomach with your arms hanging over the edge and then your legs sticking out from the end of the bed."

"That is how I was able to sleep," said Louis quietly nodding his head. "So what else did you see?"

"You did not acknowledge any of us in any way. You may have been in a trance, or in shock. Your eyes were open, but they looked straight ahead. Like you were blind. The color in the unburned parts of your body was strange. I knew you were a Negro, but I had no idea what your true color might be.

"Father Mary said he didn't think the deep burns were the most painful. He thought many of the nerve endings were entirely destroyed. He wanted you to drink water because you were oozing so much fluid, but you didn't want to drink it. You would only sip it once in a while.

"When Father Mary removed the sheet it stuck in many places. He brought away the sheet with skin attached to it. Fresh blood oozed from the spots left behind. You didn't make a sound. You didn't move. Finally Father Mary showed us your back. It didn't look human." I paused looking at Louis who had bowed his head. I had not meant to embarrass the man.

Louis raised his head when I stopped talking. He said, "It still does not look human. It is the part of me most marked. So you are right to say this and it tells me you are honest and I can believe what you say. Please to go on now."

Before I could continue we heard a noise at the door. Both of us turned our attention to the large woman coming into the shack with a tray of food, which she placed, on Louis' bed. The tray held two steaming cups of coffee, a large bowl of bananas, mangoes, pineapple and breadfruit, two bowls of mashed sweet potatoes and one plate with something that appeared to be dried fish. The woman and Louis spoke to each other briefly, and then Louis indicated that I could have one bowl of potatoes and a cup of coffee. If I wanted, I might also have a banana. The plate and everything else was for Louis.

The woman helped me sit up with my back to the wall and my legs spread out in front of me the length of the bed. The light blanket was still draped over my body. I faced straight ahead through the open door in this uncomfortable position. My back started to hurt as soon as I leaned against the wall, but the glimpse of sunshine and the chance to eat helped ease my discomfort. I took the bowl of sweet potatoes from Louis gratefully. I had never tasted anything so welcome, so tasty, so nurturing.

"So we will eat and I will let you rest while I walk and get back strength. After you rest, you will tell me what Father Mary saw of the eruption. Then you can tell me what the other scientist saw, what you saw in the city, and what you learned from the sailors and the newspaper. So only when you are finished will I tell you what I did and why I want to know everything you know about this disaster."

"I feel like Scheherazade telling the stories of the Arabian Nights," I laughed.

"What are you talking about, Edward?"

"Scheherazade was a woman who told her husband a different story every night for one thousand and one nights so he wouldn't kill her."

"So that is a good thing to remember. That you feel like Scheherazade and you can tell me more later today. You must tell me all of your stories, or you might die like that woman."

He left the room with a smile on his face. I wasn't smiling. He had just threatened to kill me if I didn't tell him everything he wanted to know.

CHAPTER SEVEN

I felt content after my first solid food and a good nap. Then the dark shadow of Louis Ciparis fell across the threshold of the shack.

"So Edward you are awake and I am back from my walk for exercise. It is time for you to talk," he said sternly. "I myself must hear what Father Mary and the scientist saw," he insisted with a rising voice. "Tell me now, please." The contrast between the stern and even vicious command and the ending "please" was frightening. I wondered just what kind of a dual personality Louis had.

"I asked Father Mary what he saw of the eruption," I began. "He said 'It was terrible, appalling. I've never seen anything like it.' Then he brought his hands together, palm to palm with the fingers touching, like he was going to pray. After a long pause he began talking slowly, quietly.

"He said a black vapor descended from the side of the mountain and enveloped the city. The upper surface of this vapor - this cloud - was like an immense plain. A heaving, rolling-plain of plowed earth. It was as if all Martinique was sliding into the sea.

"Above the volcano, there were rocket-like bursts of gray smoke then an enormous tongue of fire detached itself from the vapor and flowed into the city. Fire engulfed the British Government Residence and every building around it. Only the towers of the Cathedral of St. Pierre were untouched at first. The horrible evil fiery mass enveloped them too. It spread itself over all St. Pierre. He knew there were many victims, and from Morne Rouge there was nothing he could do. He said he did pray for the souls of the people of St. Pierre. That was all he could do.

"I asked him if he heard any noise during the eruption. He wasn't sure. He said that watching the destruction was such a powerful, compelling experience; he focused on that and nothing else. He said he would like to forget what he saw. It haunted his sleep. In time he would forget the sight. It would grow less intense with each day, but he would not forget the people who died. He would pray for them each day."

I stopped and looked at Louis intently waiting for a response. The atmosphere was somber. Louis was looking at the far wall, expressionless. There was no way to know what was going on in his mind. I wasn't sure if I had given Louis the answer he was after.

When Louis realized I was looking at him, he said, "So I need to know more. Next tell me what the science man said."

"Which one? There were two of them. One from Precheur and one from France."

"The one from Precheur first. You know," Louis paused, "that is the village, the very place, where I was born. Please to go on."

I began again, "Roger Arnoux is a member of the Astronomical Society of France. He lives in St. Pierre and he was very anxious to talk to me. It was as if the more he talked about the eruption the more he came to terms with it. Do you know what I mean, Louis?"

"No. Tell me."

"The more he talked about it, the more he believed it happened and it wasn't his imagination or just a bad nightmare. He needed to talk to make what he saw real. He saw it. He knew it was real, but he was still so stunned that he didn't believe it was real."

"I can understand this Edward. I know it was real, but I still do not want to believe it. Please to go on with your story."

At last, I was on the right track in giving Louis the information he was after. I began again. "Dr. Arnoux wanted to start from the beginning. He said he was the only survivor of all of the society members who lived in St. Pierre, including his brother. His entire family was lost. His father, his mother, his sister, his brother, all of them died because they stayed in St. Pierre. His own survival was a matter of pure luck because he went to property he owned in Parnasse, to see better what was happening with the volcano. This was the only thing that saved him.

"He became quite upset while he was talking, so Father Mary insisted we have lunch. After lunch, his composure regained, Arnoux began talking about the eruption again.

"He said he saw the first eruption from Mont Parnasse. I asked him where Parnasse was and he told me it was a high hill about two miles east of St. Pierre. He said it isn't so grand as Morne Rouge, or as cool, or as far from St. Pierre.

"He described a yellow-white vapor from the crater that went four or five thousand feet high then drifted slowly with the steady trade winds. A black cloud with a rolling motion followed this. This must be the same one Father Mary saw. He said no trace of flame was visible with this cloud. The wind was so strong that the trees bent over to the ground. On higher slopes, ash coated leaves and small branches were torn from the trees and violently thrown all around. Then there were glowing rock strata spreading around the volcano. It looked like a collar. The summit had vapors of violet and gray. Tornadic air currents swept the vapors upward. He said it was beautiful at first.

"He said he knew that Pelee was on the verge of total eruption, but he could not foresee just how devastating that eruption would be. He said he wept as the monster seemed to want to come near.

"There was a terrible wind that threatened to knock him down and he was four miles away from the volcano! Can you imagine such a wind?" Louis shook his head. No, he could not imagine such a wind. He nodded for me to continue.

"Finally it was completely dark, except for the glow from the cloud that approached St. Pierre from the north. There were three or four explosions, like canon sounds. After the sounds, there was what he called volcanic lightening. Then there was a column of inky black vapor, like a shaft of solid ebony, rising rapidly and fired with electrical charges. The eruption threw stones large enough to kill someone into the yard of the Military Hospital in Fort-de-France. That was all he had to say about what he saw of the eruption. He did talk some more about what information he was going to send to the academy in France."

"So Edward was there anything important in the information he sent to France? Anything that I should know?"

"Louis, I don't know what it is you are trying to find out, so how can I possibly know if it is important?"

"So maybe you should just tell me."

"I don't remember it all. Can you bring me my notes from my bag? I wrote his story in English, but I can translate it for you."

Louis got up and walked to a small table that held my papers. He brought them back and threw them on my lap. "So tell me," he snapped.

"Dr, Arnoux said he would start his report at an earlier date. He would go back two years and start with Pentecost Monday, 1900. With his brother, Charles, he climbed to the top of Mont Pelee with guides. They found two very small sulfur jets that had opened on the actual crater site of what is called the dry lake. They saw that for thirty to forty meters minerals had leveled trees and yellowish material, which they took to be sulfur, littered the ground. In previous climbs they always had found the richest vegetation in this area.

"The following year he went with some friends to this same place. They found five or six small craters, or jets, giving off a very green, nasty-looking smoke, which reeked of sulfur. He said it wasn't until March of this year that this phenomenon appeared in any appreciable form for anyone to notice in St. Pierre.

"He said the residents around the heights of Precheur told of smelling sulfur almost continually. A friend of his, who lived in Morne Orange, told him that one night during the end of March he saw a bright light coming from the bottom of the crater. The weather was cloudy during the whole of April and no one realized the extent of what was happening inside the mountain. The residents of Precheur said they had heard explosions, others said they had saw fire. It wasn't until the night of April 25th anyone believed that the volcano had started to erupt again.

"He went to bed about 11:30 the night of April 25th. He woke up to a very strong explosion, which he thought was thunder. The same noise happened again only a minute later. He got up to look at the sky thinking it was rather strange to have a storm in April. As soon as he looked at the mountain, he knew an eruption was taking place. He looked where he knew the crater was. He could see an immense column of smoke heading northeast. Explosions and rumblings continued, while a vapor column, or steam column, sent out sparks. At that point, coarse gray sand began to fall in a thickness of half a centimeter. This gray sand fell as thick as buckshot.

"The eruption lasted until about 1:30 in the morning. It seemed to slow down, only to start again towards 5:00. This time it threw up light gray sand with finer grains.

"On the following days, they noticed a large gray-blue cloud, which looked like a regular storm cloud, on the mountain. There were no rumblings, no storm. They thought the crater had opened and that things were going to get worse.

"On the morning of May 2nd, about 9:00, the same symptoms of the first eruption happened again. There were explosions, rumblings, ash, etc. He noticed the crater had grown larger and two other small craters were opening very close to the original crater in the area of the dry lake.

"It wasn't until May 5th that the crater began to erupt and flow down, through the River Blanche. This flow was made up of very strong thick waves of a black mud topped by very dense steam. This lava completely buried the Guerin factory and the workers." I paused and glanced at Louis, "I read the same description in Les Colonies. It must have been frightening for the people."

"I know many workers at that sugar factory. So they are gone now, washed away in black mud lava from the evil volcano." Louis sighed. We sat quietly on our beds. Finally Louis broke the heavy silence, "They run fast, my friends at the factory. So it must be very quick, this lava, to catch them. So please to go on."

I started reading my notes again. "The next day was May 6th and the eruption seemed to calm down. The steam escaping from the crater didn't have as much force. They thought the eruption and lava flow were subsiding.

"On the 7th of May, in the morning, he was in the Berte rum factory speaking with the telegraph service director who told him all telegraph communication between Martinique and other islands was dead. The director had the idea the loss of the telegraph services occurred because of certain depressions under the ocean. It was at this point that the thought of some type of catastrophe crossed Mr. Arnoux's mind.

"In the afternoon, in St. Pierre, they heard explosions coming every so often from the south. There was a strange vibration in the air that made things tremble on the shelves. People said there was a ship on maneuvers in the waters of Fort-de-France. A battleship somewhere in the south was causing the movement.

"He left St. Pierre, towards 5:00 and witnessed a spectacle when the crater threw enormous rocks very high in the air. It took about 15 seconds for the rocks to fall to the ground. These same rocks were thrown well over the top of the highest point of the plateau.

"Towards 8:00, he saw strong continuous white flames coming from the top of the crater. Shortly after, there was the same type of explosions coming from the south that he heard earlier. This confirmed his idea that underground craters were releasing gas that exploded on contact with air.

"This night he went to bed towards 9:00 and woke up shortly in a suffocating heat, completely covered with sweat. All the events had disturbed his nerves and he thought he was falling ill. He went back to bed.

"An earthquake woke him up at 11:35. No one in the house woke up. He thought it was his nerves again and went back to bed.

"The next morning, May 8th, he woke up at 7:30. He looked out the window toward the crater. He thought it was rather calm. Steam was coming out quickly and there was a wind blowing from the east. Toward 8:00 he looked at the crater again.

"This time he saw a small wave of steam followed about two seconds later by a very large wave which took fewer than three seconds to cover the Point de Carbet. At the same time, it was heading their way and getting thicker, higher and wider. There was steam coming out from everywhere. This steam was identical to the steam that was coming out of the crater. It was of a gray-violet color and looked very dense. This wave was continually rounded and steam kept coming out of it. From the steam there also came innumerable electric sparks. This whole time there was a deafening noise coming out of the crater.

"This was when he knew that St. Pierre was pulverized and completely destroyed. He says he began to cry for his family, his belongings, everything he had left in St. Pierre. As this monster seemed to be getting close to them, all his terrified servants began to run to the top of a small hill above the house. They begged him to do the same.

"This is when a terrible wind came. It shook the leaves off the trees and broke branches off. They fought the wind to get to the top of this little hill. When they got to the top, the sun disappeared. Everything became completely black. Stones began to fall. The largest stone was about two centimeters.

"At this same time, they saw a column of fire which seemed to be undulating and rotating. It had to be at least 400 meters high. This lasted maybe two to three minutes. Then stones rained again. Then came a rain of mud that leveled all the trees and bushes. Finally came a torrential rain, which lasted about half an hour.

"The entire phenomenon lasted about an hour. Then the sun shown through again. Dr. Arnoux stopped talking. His voice was quivering. He paused to compose himself. Father Mary and myself remained silent to give him time to put his thoughts in order. After all this man had been through, the least we could do was give him our silent respect. We waited patiently for him to speak. When he did start to talk again, his voice was strong and composed.

He said "The wave he saw over St. Pierre must have been composed of a liquid at a very high temperature. This turned to steam on contact with the air. Not instantly, but a second or two later. This is the only way he could explain it. It is hard to conceive a gas that has two opposing forces, the force of falling and the force of rising all in the same gas.

"He thought lightning had to have some type of contribution to the fire, since the steam was producing electric sparks as it rose. As this gas was escaping, it must have produced a vacuum. This would have asphyxiated all the people who lived in St. Pierre, and would have killed anyone who wasn't already dead from the lava flow."

"Edward, what does this mean asphyxiated?"

"It means the gas produced a vacuum that would keep the people from breathing." He nodded he understood. "Please to go on, Edward."

"Dr. Arnoux went on to explain the terrible wind caused by the vacuum, the wind he felt in Parnasse, must have finished off the city. He did not observe the rain of fire that many people in Carbet talked about, but he did observe the eruption from start to finish. He has never seen anything like it.

"He thought the volcanic material, that is ash, mud and stones, which fell on Fort-de-France, and fell on practically the whole island, must have come from some kind of dome thrown out by the crater several seconds after the destruction of St. Pierre. He did not see the expected vertical eruption. The steam that fell on St. Pierre in a couple of seconds completely covered Martinique. He himself believes that this gas was simply a matter of hot water and high temperature. Shortly after the eruption and for a long time, he was able to smell a very strong odor of what he called boiled earth. That was all he had to say."

Louis was quiet for a few minutes then said, "So that is what burned me then. Steam. I want you to tell me about the city next and about the other person you met there."

"It would help if I knew what you wanted me to say."

"No. I am most sad I cannot tell you. You must tell me everything, then I will know my question has been answered."

I wondered just how much more I could remember to tell Louis. When would this end?

CHAPTER EIGHT

"Now I must learn what you saw at St. Pierre." Louis looked at me intensely. "Remember you must be honest with me. If it was ugly, you must tell me ugly."

"Louis, I'm not sure where to start. It was ugly. St. Pierre was extinct. It had a shroud of gray ash, something appropriate to the dead," I began reluctantly. I continued after a brief pause to gather my thoughts. Just how much could I tell him?

"The silence was unearthly. Desolation and a feeling of intense loneliness surrounded me there. Everything was forsaken, forgotten, forbidding. It was chilling to see, incomprehensible. I wondered what happened to the spirited city, the friendly people, and the energy of carnival? I wondered if this devastation, this jumble of ash and rocks, really was the city that once entranced me?

"I must confess, the emptiness before me was numbing." I paused reflectively for a few minutes. "I don't like feeling this way. I pride myself on being immune to emotion, but in my wildest imagination I hadn't expected such desolation. There was nothing to greet me. No color. No form. No life. Only loneliness, stillness, grayness and emptiness. There was simply rubble left of what had been the bright, sparkling, friendly city.

"I looked over the disaster and estimated the destruction covered about eight square miles, all focused on St. Pierre. There was absolutely nothing to show a vibrant city, this jewel other cities were jealous of, ever existed. The eruptions completely destroyed her.

"The fountain in the Place Bertin was still flowing after the first eruption, but now not even that powerful fountain was left standing. I had the feeling that no one would ever rebuild here because there were no people to rebuild and no reason for it.

"I was in an empty, desolate ruin in a place that should have been perfect. I never saw a catastrophe like this before. I looked for a common theme with other disasters I had seen, something to convey to other people the awfulness of it. But I couldn't tell what that theme was.

"The only thing that came to my mind was Macbeth talking about man's insignificance. '...*Tomorrow and tomorrow, creeps in this petty pace from day to day, to the last syllable of recorded time; And all our yesterdays have lighted fools the way to dusty death. Out, out brief candle! Life's but a walking shadow, a poor player that struts and frets his hour upon the stage, and then is heard no more; it is a tale told by an idiot, full of sound and fury, signifying nothing.'*

"Edward, what does this mean, this Macbeth?" Louis looked perplexed.

"Macbeth is a play written by Shakespeare, a famous English writer. Shakespeare is suggesting life is full of noise and anger and doesn't mean anything. That man is easily destroyed. I thought of this because in St. Pierre thirty thousand people were killed in a matter of seconds."

Louis repeated, "Life is noisy and hot-tempered and has no meaning." He paused in thought. "So, Edward, is this true?"

"Some people believe so, Louis."

"So do you believe it?"

"I don't know. Do you?"

"That is part of what I am deciding. So we must talk about this much more. Please to go on, Edward."

I reflected for a moment on the absolute shocking desolation, and then I started talking again. "The ruins were so silent, I imagined sounds and where buildings stood. Using the barest outlines of the streets and foundations, I thought I could remember some patterns. Because of the close building of houses, one on the other, to keep heat out, I always saw the city as a closely packed beehive of life.

"The loss was so awful, it stunned me. I couldn't act on anything. I wasn't moving. I wasn't exploring. I knew I had to get a grip on myself. I couldn't just stand there dumbfounded. This was, after all, work, an assignment. It offered me a chance to assure my position as a leading feature writer, and so I reasoned myself out of my inaction. I reminded myself that I had nothing to mourn, this was not my home, and I had lost nothing. I could get to work.

"There was no street that I could remember being absolutely straight or absolutely flat. As you know the streets curved and twisted and suddenly went off at an angle. They would climb and sink. No streets, or even the stones to mark them, were left in place.

"Before, you could hear the sound of water running through the gutters at the edge of all the sidewalks. Besides the running water, the city also had an abundance of shade trees along the stone paved streets and in gardens. No running water or trees were left.

"The day I landed was a clear, perfect tropical day, which made the scene before me even worse. I remembered those crazy winding streets and the multitude of bridges crossing the many streams. As a lad, I counted twenty-five streams. Did you ever count them, Louis?"

"No. There is no reason to count streams." Louis looked at me and shook his head. "But you remember this? So what else do you remember?"

"I remember the colorful city vividly because it is not like anything in the United States. The houses were a bright yellow or orange with peaked red roofs and dormers painted yellow. The windows were frame, without glass, but had shutters painted blue or green. Those shutters were fun to play with because they had wooden slats that moved to let light and air into a room. When you closed them, they kept the room cool and cut out noise and they offered protection from bothersome insects.

"I enjoyed the babbling sound that was everywhere from the running water of all the streams. To have so much water running through a city was also unusual to me. Having this abundance of water, the city blossomed with tropical plants and trees. Hibiscus, anthurium, bougainvillea and wild orchids flourished. The water and warmth encouraged greens so compelling they were unearthly. Do you appreciate what you had here?" I asked Louis.

"So I did not think any of this was special and it is good to hear you tell me what made it remarkable. Please to go on now."

"The crazy sidewalks were enough to bring a smile to anyone's face because they varied so much in width. They were either a foot wide or three feet wide. The sidewalks were as unpredictable as the streets."

"You truly did like my city. You did feel it was special." Louis smiled at me. "I did not know it was so special. Now I think maybe it was. Please to do on, Edward."

"I glanced along what had been the southern edge of the city, the mooring place, the Mouillage. There had been long, cobbled quays running almost to the Carbet River, then the village of Carbet. Now there was devastation as far as the eye could see.

"The breeze reminded me that a curve of land sheltered the harbor from strong winds. This remains. I remember the warm air was usually rich with the scents of sugar, cinnamon, and rum. Or, sometimes, not often thank goodness, it smelled of garlic. Those smells were gone. Only burned ash and some sulfur smell was left.

"It had been a beautiful, lush city. Now, there wasn't a tree standing upright. There were no bridges. There were no streams for the bridges to cross. The milky iridescence of the River Blanch was gone. The noisy, turbulent, shallow Roxelane that cut through the center district was gone. All signs of civilization were erased. No riverbanks marked where the rivers had been.

"I was in an empty, desolate ruin in a place that should have been perfect. I was feeling melancholy when I heard someone calling me. The unexpected sound of another voice made me flinch. The noise this greeting made booming through this wasteland was unbelievable. I turned and saw two men coming toward me.

"I shouted back to acknowledge them. One of the men was a barefoot, white trousered native, like yourself, and the other was a pith helmeted outsider like myself. The men approached me cautiously, picking their way through the ruins and searching for signs that something had once lived here.

"The man introduced himself as Henri Duvall, a scientist from France, and with him was a helper, Auguste, a Martinican from Carbet. He said they were exploring the ruins for scientific information.

"He invited me to join them for lunch and told me that after he explored the ruins he was going to Morne Rouge, where there was a survivor. That was the first I heard of you. It was absolutely amazing to me that someone survived this terrible eruption.

"He told me that more than one survived the eruption. There were four survivors, but you are the only who was still alive.

"We stood silently looking at the volcano. It seemed like she was still guarding her prize by sending up offerings of smoke, the only thing that moved in the wasteland.

"When we walked into the rubble, we found three-foot thick walls torn to pieces like dominoes. The nine to ten-foot long six-inch guns in the battery were dismounted. The large statue of the Virgin Mary was forty to fifty feet away from her pedestal. That statue must weigh two or three tons but it looked like a giant child's hand moved it aside as if it were tired of play.

"We saw a tarantula that must have found a cool place to hide its small body. Henri said the people were not so lucky. They found an unusual number of bodies at street intersections. Of course, many sought shelter in the shadow of the Cathedral cross.

"He reminded me that people are made of water. They can vaporize. In purely basic terms this indicated to him that most of the victims boiled to death. The fortunate ones died from inhalation of the hot gas. He does not think any of them suffered. It was all too quick."

Obviously disturbed, Louis got up and walked to the doorframe. Leaning against it he took a few deep breaths. "Please to go on, Edward."

"Henri pointed out the fallen trees saying you can see from how the trees fell that it was a horizontal blast from Pelee. It was a horizontal blast of hot dust that caused the fires.

"He said it was reasonable to presume that not all the people died instantly. There was fire throughout the city so there was no escape for any that survived the initial eruption. If trapped, they would have been badly burned or roasted to death. Most bodies were not identifiable. The heat was so great that the steamer Marin couldn't get near St. Pierre until 11:30 that morning."

Louis stretched his hands out to grasp the frame while he stood looking out from the open doorway. He threw his head back taking a deep breath of air. He turned to look back into the room at me. "For me hearing this is very painful, but I must hear all you know to make my decision. Please to go on."

"Louis, if you tell me what your decision is about I might be able to help you better. I'll tell you what you need to know exactly instead of just talking on and on about the eruption. You don't need to know everything I know. Just tell me about the decision you are trying to make."

"No," said Louis emphatically. He walked back to his bed with an air of purpose. "I told you it was a matter of living or dying. It is your job to tell me what I want to know. It is not your business to help me make any decisions. So please to go on," Louis directed sternly.

I started talking again with some reluctance. "When I interviewed the survivors of the Roraima in Fort-de-France, they told me that after the eruption there was a period of total darkness. Henri confirmed this. He said people in Carbet, who were closest, told him it was like the obscurity of a windowless cellar or a deep cave. The part of Carbet where he was staying was also dark. When the sun came out, in about half an hour, it was like a red ball in a smoky haze. St. Pierre was on fire.

"The heat was incredible. Searchers in the ruins found melted silver in a safe and fused to the steel case. They also found drinking glasses melted together, yet untouched crockery was sitting next to the glasses. He said he saw completely untouched crockery, placed as if freshly laid out for a meal.

"Henri told me they found many freakish effects. He said most of the victims found outside didn't have clothes on. The passing hurricane wind must have simply whipped the clothes off the bodies. It amazed him that fragile or combustible objects were untouched, but larger, solid objects became fragmented or were consumed completely.

"They found rice and coffee carbonized in the bowls. Books with blackened leaves. Singed checks, drawn on the Bank of France, that were not burned, just singed. Then they found an iron-spiked fence that had melted. They found keys to doors. The doors were gone, but the keys remained. Wedding rings were blackened. An undamaged sewing machine was near a pile of fused screws. There was a blackened flute with melted keys and a horribly twisted trumpet.

"He told me about finding six glasses, nested together and fused. Can you picture this Louis? Six glasses nesting, one within the other, all melted together? How capricious!"

"So I can picture this, but what is capricious?"

"Unpredictable, inconsistent," I paused. There had to be a better way to describe this that Louis would understand. "Hit or miss," I said with a satisfied smile directed at Louis.

"So please to go on."

My satisfaction short lived, I sighed and started talking again. "He said they found twisted bars of iron and sheathing from the roofs curved around posts like a piece of cloth. But they also found little cups of china that were perfect. Some bottles had their corks still in them and held pure water. The corks did not expand or burst. The bottles were perfect. The water was still good. Do you understand?" Louis nodded he understood.

I continued, "They found a bundle of clay pipes, the clay was not burned. Some of the thick house-front walls, three or four-feet thick walls, crumbled up and blew away, just like a house built with a pack of cards.

"I think I've told you everything about the city."

"So that is everything you saw and everything the man Henri told you?"

I paused thoughtfully. How much more could he tell Louis? "He did tell me a little more about how the people died and about the prison where you were found."

"Then tell me that," ordered Louis.

"He said steam is not hot enough to kill instantly. It would scald the flesh under clothing. Perhaps this is what happened to you, Louis."

"Perhaps," Louis replied quietly.

"Henri also said the hot dust would set fire to anything that could burn and the dust could get in everywhere. Since there were no windows in St. Pierre, only openings with shutters, the dust could enter there. The houses burned from the inside out.

"When he told me about the prisons, he said French prisons aren't like American ones. Prisoners themselves run the French prisons. There are very little administrative personnel. The trustees are prisoners and run everything. The kitchen, hospital, laundry, work parties, everything to do with the prison. At night it is completely locked up. Then with the wardens in the guardhouse, the prison is secure. It is society by itself."

"This is true, Edward. This prison system is part of why I am alive."

"How is that, Louis?"

"No. You do not trick me. I will not answer your questions until you have answered mine. First I must hear what the sailors told you and what you read in the newspapers."

"Aren't you getting a little tired of hearing this?"

Louis looked at me with a scowl. "So, are you crazy? You are telling me how my people died. How my life has been destroyed." Louis was angry. He slapped at the bed as he got up to leave. "I tell you this is a matter of living or dying and you will tell me everything

you know." He stormed out of the shack leaving me stunned.

CHAPTER NINE

"Good morning," a smiling, alert Louis greeted me as I stretched and wiped sleep from my eyes and yawned. "This will be an exciting day for you Edward. Today you get up and walk."

I chuckled quietly to myself. "Louis, do you honestly believe I can get up and walk just as if nothing had happened? Like everything is normal for me and this is another usual, ordinary day in my life? You're telling me I can overlook that I've been in bed so long and just get up and walk? I don't think so."

"Yes, you can. So I have seen other men do this before. Truly, I have seen others who have been in bed a long time. Longer than you. They get up and walk. The women gave you food for strength and they exercised your arms and legs for you. You will shake and be most often unsteady first, but after you will get better and better at walking. So you can get up and walk. Trust me. Try it now." Louis extended his hand to me to help me get up.

I took his hand reluctantly for two reasons. I did not believe I could stand up and walk and I was also hesitant because of the delicate look of Louis' healing skin. I did not want to open the skin by putting pressure on it. But since Louis didn't give me any choice, I took the extended hand, trying not to tax the strength of his hand or create tension on the new skin. Slowly, unsure of myself, I stood up.

"So I told you so. See you can do it," said Louis with a smile. "Now walk."

Getting on my feet was far easier than I expected. With results like this, my medical treatment was quite impressive. Since I got up, maybe I could walk. Then I noticed women in the small hut. They were watching me closely. Much to my embarrassment, they did not avert their eyes as my light covering slipped from my naked body. I had the feeling they had been waiting for this very occurrence. They were looking directly at me quite pointedly. With a laugh, Louis handed me a breechcloth.

Because I was stiff, it was very awkward for me to put the breechcloth on. My legs did not bend the way I wanted them to. I did not want to sit down to dress because I was afraid I didn't have the energy to get up again. I struggled and clumsily got the bit of fabric on my body, barely keeping my balance.

Louis laughed at me. "You will get your own clothes when we are ready to leave," he said trying to suppress further laughter. "So you are upset because the women are watching you while you are naked."

I felt foolish nodding yes, but it did make me uncomfortable. I wasn't sure why. I didn't consider myself to be modest in any extreme. I was not a Puritan after all.

A sly smile flitted across Louis' face again. "Do not let this upset you. They have seen you all naked before. Your body is nothing that shames you. For a white man, you are adequate." He laughed, leaving me feeling uneasy. His moment of mirth exhausted, Louis said, "Remember these women took turns caring for you. I tell you, they have seen you. All of you. You, a naked defenseless white man. That is a rare sight for these women. Now they are talking and deciding how much fun you might be at bamboche. Now, having seen you, maybe they all want you. So they are fighting about you. You have nothing to be ashamed of."

I thought how irritating it was to have Louis go from laughing at me to mocking me by pretending to be serious about such personal matters. Maybe Louis was serious. From what I knew of Louis, he did not have the temperament to tease people, nor the wit to be subtle about it. It was hard to understand why Louis smiled and laughed so often. This man had to have deep psychological wounds, yet outwardly he was all smiles.

I'll play his game, I decided. "All of them want me?" I asked quite seriously as I moved uncertainly to the door on my wooden legs with help from Louis. "All of them? Even Marie?"

"Maybe especially Marie. She did a grand amount of work for you. She showed everyone how to exercise your legs while you were not with us. Now you can walk, and soon you will walk like never in bed. I told you that you could. Marie spoon-fed you rich broth and special secret teas to make you strong and bring your mind back to you. She was the one to first undress you and clean you. She made sure you were clean every day. I believe she liked what she saw. So she may like you very much. She has never had a white man before that she has talked about. This puts a great burden on your shoulders." With a laugh Louis slapped me on the back in an unusual display of energy.

This embarrassed me again. Even in college they were not so open with their remarks. Men were always more discrete.

"How is enjoying a woman like Marie a burden?" I asked attempting to overcome my discomfort.

"Ah, but it is a burden, it is. If you do not love her to her satisfaction, do not give her full enjoyment, she will never permit another white man her pleasures. She will think that all white men are inadequate lovers. She is not all that generous with black men, but I have hope because she also cared for me. She healed my burns."

"Yes, Louis. She did take care of you and your healing is astounding to me. Marie did an unbelievable thing. How could you have healed so quickly? It doesn't seem possible that your burns have healed. Are you sure you can be out in the sun without it hurting you? Are you entirely healed?"

Louis answered, "I am not entirely healed. But that is not what we are talking about. I do not know if all the women want you. Sometime I will ask them. For now Marie told me we should walk and rest. Then walk again, a little longer, then rest. Each time we walk it is for a little longer. We should be strong by the end of the day and there is a healing ceremony for us tonight."

"What is a healing ceremony?"

"So it is to be sure for certain we continue to get well, in body and in our spirit. Do you understand? Let me explain it this way. It protects us from losing what we have gotten in healing so far and to get better and better."

"Louis, I can't walk without my shoes."

"Why not?"

"I have never walked without my shoes. My feet are always protected."

Louis spoke to the one woman left in the shack and gestured at Edward's feet. She answered, and he turned back to Edward. "So she says your feet were too soft and they put a special salve on them to make them normal. You can walk without a problem."

"No, Louis I can't. I have never gone barefoot."

"Why not?"

I had to think about this a minute. Why not? I wanted to, many times. "Because my parents would never let me, even here on the island," I answered.

"So your parents are not here." Louis was plainly disgusted at the answer. "Let us go now."

Emerging from the shack, I confirmed what I thought. It was a typical native dwelling, with a dirt floor, and a roof of sugar cane leaves. There was a small garden with eggplant and onion and chickens running through it. A little ways away were some fruit trees, orange, grapefruit and lime.

The hut was at the edge of a sugar can field on one side and a natural forest area on the other. The lush green growth was so thick, I could not see through it. On the forest side of the hut I could hear the sound of waves washing a beach, but I could see nothing of the water.

We started by walking in a small circle around the hut, stopped for a short rest and then circled it again. It was another beautiful crystal clear day and the comfort of the warm soft breeze and the island aromas of sweet orchids made it a pleasure to walk, no matter how uncertainly.

"Is the ocean through the trees?" I asked.

"Yes. We will be able to go there in one day. When we walk and rest you tell me about what you learned from the newspapers. Please to keep talking now. Talk about the newspapers."

"They gave me the newspapers in order by the day they were published. That way I could go through them and see what happened when. I wanted to see what the clues were before this horrendous eruption, if the people had any warning. And I found that they did have warnings, but ignored them." Thinking I had said enough, I stopped talking.

"So, Edward, this is not enough. Tell me exactly what you found," Louis insisted.

"It was not pretty. Are you sure you want to hear it?"

"Do not make me angry, Edward. So I told you I wanted to hear it."

"It would be easier if I had my notes."

"No, Edward, just tell me what you remember. That will be enough for now." Louis was clearly losing patience.

"I started reading early April newspapers. The headline said something like Mont Pelee Talks. It was the report of low rumbling sounds coming from the volcano. Sharp tremors were felt as well. This let the people know that the volcano would not be ignored and a scouting party set out to have a look. This scouting party discovered new lava filling the crater floor which everyone thought was good news. After all, there was plenty of room in the volcano for lava.

"The last week of April the paper talked about the ash coming from Pelee. This article reported the volcano had begun coughing up ashes and sulfurous gases. Birds died. Horses hooves made no noise on the ash-covered street. Sometimes the disturbed ashes suffocated them. People put wet handkerchiefs over their faces for protection."

"This I remember, Edward. It is hard to believe such a thing when the air is so pure and sweet today. People who always cough had a very hard time. I think some people died also and not just horses. Please to go on now."

"Next the Roxelane River turned into a surge of mud through the center of town. This was sometime the first few days of May. This mud knocked out the power plant and telegraph lines. Halfway up the slope of the volcano a fissure opened and destroyed the village of Ajoupa-Bouillon, the buildings and the people, about one hundred and sixty lives I think. Then steam and boiling mud came from the fissures and pumice stone and ash rained on the city.

"I do remember more, but it is hard to walk and talk. I am getting out of breath."

Louis was not sympathetic. "So talk slower," he growled at me.

"The paper said the fine ash drove the cleaning women crazy. They couldn't get rid of it. It kept coming. It got into cracks and inside drawers. It filtered into everything, everywhere. Nothing worked to clean it away.

"Businesses closed because no one could get through the ash to do trade except on foot. No carriages or cars. Officials declared a school holiday, which made sense because the schools were empty anyway.

"You know what bothers me Louis it the editorials in Les Colonies said there was nothing to worry about. They newspaper reported that Father Roche, who knew about volcanoes had the situation. He said that the formation would send the lava away from St. Pierre. People could come to the city for safety."

"This does not surprise me. So I would believe the good priest. He is an educated man."

"In spite of everything that was happening, you would believe him?" I was perplexed.

Louis answered sharply, "Yes, I told you I would believe the priest. A priest does not lie about such things. Of course I would believe him. Please to go on, Edward."

"Next came flooding. It was reported that just before one o'clock that day, I think it was May 5, the sea retreated a hundred meters, then rushed back in a matter of minutes to flood the Mouillage District. Many drowned. They thought a wave made of steam, dust and gas from the volcano triggered this.

"They reported the hot mud and gas drove insects and fer-de-lances ahead of it. That is why I feel so foolish not thinking about the dangers before I even went to St. Pierre let alone driving a mule back down the Eastern coast."

"Edward, we know there was nothing to do for us. It does not make any sense to go over what cannot be changed. So please to go on now."

"The steaming mud river formed in all this mess was huge. It destroyed the entire Guerin sugar plantation and all the workers. The mud surged into the ocean, creating huge waves and flooding the downtown section where more people drowned.

"Next Soufriere, the volcano on St. Vincent erupted. Everybody seemed to think this was good news. The reasoning was if Soufriere erupted, then there would be less pressure under the other islands, like Martinique."

"Edward, you look unhappy about this. It makes sense to me."

"I am unhappy Louis. It doesn't make sense. It's saying the two volcanoes are connected so the islands are connected some way. It made people think St. Pierre was safer when it wasn't."

"So please to go on, Edward."

"The Governor, Mouttet, decided to come. When Mouttet visited St. Pierre, I think it was May 7; he wanted to see for himself what was happening. Remember there was no electric power in the city, muddy little streams ran everywhere, streets were full of debris and a fine gray dust covered everything. On top of this, homeless refugees were coming from the country because St. Pierre was safer. Mouttet opened the military barracks to the refugees because people were leaving, but more were coming in. He also canceled the Annual Ascension Day Ball. Surely that should have been a signal something was wrong?"

"No, Edward. This makes sense to me. The city is crowded and unclean with dust so a ball is not important. What happened next?"

"Pelee was growling and lightning came from her summit. Two craters glowed red. Debris from the volcano washed down in torrents of black water. The paper reported that even with this, the governor reassured everyone; everything would be fine. The fissures opening along the slopes meant that the volcanic power was draining.

"Then came the eruption on May 8 at precisely 7:52 a.m. I know that because that is when the telegraph communications from St. Pierre to Fort-de-France stopped. A few minutes later the people in Fort-de-France saw a black mushroom of smoke rising above Mont Pelee. This smoke moved rapidly, six or seven miles a minute. And that is the story of the eruption."

"Governor Mouttet also died then, didn't he, Edward?"

"Yes, he did."

"So why do I feel that is as it should be?"

"In my country, Louis, we call something like this poetic justice, meaning it is something the man deserved by believing his own stories."

"So I like this poetic justice idea.

We walked silently and concentrated on completing the circle again. We continued to walk through the trees, some with romantic-looking hanging moss. We walked in ever-increasing circles until the women called us to eat. We had brief nap after eating and then began walking our circles once more.

Now we walked in silence. Both of us enjoyed the splendid day. I pointed out a humming bird and we fell silent again. It was unspoken, but we checked for snakes as we proceeded. We walked cautiously in ever widening circles through the edge of the forest until we reached the cane field on one side and the ocean on the other.

Late in the day we went back to the shack with more strength than we had left with. This amazed me. The women called us back for another rest before the evening meal. As we approached the shack, I saw a remarkable sight. I saw one of the women bathing a chicken. What a bewildering meaningless picture. Nobody washed chickens.

"What on earth is that about?" I asked Louis.

"It is special preparation for the healing ceremony."

I decided it must be some part of ritual food preparation. I remembered what Father Mary told me about the animals I had seen that evening so long ago. This chicken could be for sacrifice, with warm blood to drink. The thought was chilling to me. I didn't mind a sacrifice, after all people butchered animals for food every day. However, drinking blood was something I did not relish. I did not think I could manage it.

Hesitantly I touched Louis on the arm. "Will I have to drink blood?"

Louis looked perplexed for a moment. He glanced at the chicken and then back at me. "No," he replied. "Even if you do, it is not that bad," he added with a smile.

I deliberately put aside any thoughts of what was to come. I settled in to eat food I could recognize and a beverage I knew, water. I still didn't know what to expect at the healing ceremony. Did it include sex like *bamboche*?

CHAPTER TEN

Seeing movement in my bed, Louis called out, "So wake up. Today is the day for decisions."

"What decisions?" I asked with a yawn.

"About how soon we can have the visit from the seer and the healing ceremony. So we should be up and walking because Marie told me if we do well, we can be off to Fort-de-France soon after we see the seer and have the healing ceremony. To get a ride we will have to walk to the plantation house, so we must be in good shape to walk that far. If they have no carts going in to the city from the plantation, we may have to walk to Fort-de-France. So we have to be even stronger for that.

"You are doing well because Marie fed you rich broth and exercised your legs for you and you are strong. I am getting stronger by the hour. So get up. Let us walk to the beach and swim. We need to move about. We need to enjoy this handsome day and have it help us get strong and healthy." Louis pulled me to my feet and started walking to the door.

"I could be more enthusiastic if you said we should go for a swim." Still feeling the effects of sleep, I reluctantly joined Louis. "Can we at least have some coffee first?"

"So we can take coffee and fruit with us," said Louis.

"Are you going to be comfortable in the sun, Louis?" I was genuinely concerned even though I knew Louis had been outside before. His skin still looked like a delicate membrane, something easily destroyed.

As we went outside with our coffee cups and a bag of fruit, Louis answered, "I have a shirt to protect me when I start to feel the sun. The sun will not hurt me. I did not believe I would heal so quickly. Maybe I am meant to stay alive after all."

"You told me what Marie did for me. What did she do for you? Do you remember at all?" I asked.

"Marie put me to sleep for a few days, just like she had you sleep. So while I was sleeping, she used secret ointments on me. This salve I have now keeps the pain away. It makes me heal faster and it keeps sickness away too.

"None of the women know what she used. If she does not tell them, or will not tell them about the ointments, they try to decide what she is using by its smell. They know it included honey and sesame seeds, but it was a new smell even to them."

I admired Louis' taut shiny new skin. Even he knew the healing was phenomenal. "Louis, could you get some of the first ointment she used to heal your burns for me, and also the second one that stops itching. This is very important. I can take them to physicians and scientists, who can find out what is in them and use them for other people. What Marie is doing for you is remarkable, amazing, like a miracle. Just think of all the burned people who can use this help. The way you have healed is unbelievable, except I have seen it with my own eyes."

"So it would be most worthy to know what she is using, but no," Louis shook his head vigorously. "She will not share her secrets even in that way. So I will tell you again. Marie is powerful and this is how she keeps her power - by keeping her secrets. Besides, she makes this medicine fresh each time she uses it, and she only makes enough for one use. What you ask is not possible."

"We must find out what she uses. This is indispensable information to have. It will help many people. Are you sure there isn't a way to find out?"

"Edward, forget this idea. She will not share and no one here could tell what she was using. We do not know if it came from the trees, the animals, the ocean. We do not know and we cannot find out." We lapsed into silence as we walked toward the beach.

"You know, Edward, I think you have told me enough so now I can start to make the life or death decision."

Louis looked serious and spoke very deliberately. I felt a knot in my stomach. The day had started pleasantly; even if too soon, and here was a reminder that my life was still in question. Louis perplexed me. Burned he was weak and no threat. Healed he presented a very real danger, but how could he be so friendly one minute and so threatening the next. Maybe the man was irrational. What if I made him angry? Would that end my life quickly?

Louis looked at me. "Edward, I see distress on your face. Your mouth is tight and your forehead is wrinkled up but the sun is not in your eyes. So what is the matter with you?" he asked.

"I am concerned about this decision you are making." My voice was controlled and even. I did not want to show my alarm.

"So I still need your help to be sure I have everything in order. Even now I think about suicide, but everyone here wants to get me well and this confuses me. I feel I would betray them and what they are doing for me if I did take my own life. They do not care about me surviving the eruption, they care that I am alive now.

"Suicide makes no sense when many people care about you, so suicide is selfish but it would solve my problems. I am not truly important to these people. I am nobody to them, yet they do care for me. They are not my family. I have just met them. Why should they care?

"Some of these people feel I must be magical. They want to treat me like a God. I do not think that Marie, for one, thinks I am special because I am still alive - after two misfortunes, the volcano and the snake biting the mule and upsetting the cart. But still, I cannot think of a reason to continue to live. I am not a god."

I stood disbelieving what I heard. "This is what your decision is about? Whether you should commit suicide or not?" I asked gleefully, a look of relief flooding over me.

"So what did you think?" came Louis' sharp retort.

"I'm not sure what I thought. I guess I thought it was my life and death you were talking about."

"But Edward, why would you think that?" Louis was obviously stunned at the thought. "Where would you get that idea? I have no reason to harm you."

"That's right," I nodded my head with a smile. "You have no reason to harm me. I'm glad you have cleared up this misunderstanding. Now that I know what you are thinking of, perhaps I can really be more help to you. You want to discuss your own suicide and why you should or shouldn't do it. Right?"

"So that is exactly right. What do you think I have been saying so long to you?" Louis was puzzled. Maybe I was not the brilliant man he thought.

"You said you were a part of the voodoo community, so you are a part of something," I began feeling considerably relieved. "That must be an important reason to live. You say you can't think of a reason to live, and I've given you one. Now, can you think of any reason not to live?"

"Of course! I can think of many. I have nothing. I can do very little and I still have pain."

"Louis, it is not true that you have nothing. You have your life. It bothers me to hear you talk like this. I don't like people talking about suicide.

"Why? I have the privilege to end my life."

"First, I do not know if committing suicide is a privilege. If it is, I do not know if you, as an individual, have the privilege. This is a big philosophical question. You talk about killing yourself, which shocks me, yet you appear eager to get to Fort-de-France. I don't think I need to worry about you being serious. Don't even think about it anymore. Besides, if you die now you'll never know what happens next."

Louis laughed at the last idea. "Edward, part of me does want to know what happens next, part of me is eager to get to Fort-de-France and part of me has great fear. I do not know what waits for me there. Yet, that is the place I must go to see if any of my family survived.

The information is there to help me find any members of my family that survive in the villages. Do you have a word when part of you wants something and another equally strong part does not?"

"Yes, Louis. Not one word but two. Mixed emotions. Why did you want all of the information about the eruption?" I was curious. I had spent hours recreating the disaster for Louis because I felt personally threatened. It was hard to believe that was all for nothing.

"So you see, Edward, my past has been erased and I do not know what my future is. I cannot even imagine a future. I must live in the present, but I do not know how to live at all. I thought if I knew everything about the eruption, about the people who died, then the answer of living or dying would be easy to see," answered Louis. "It is not so easy."

We fell silent as we walked out of the sheltering palms toward the sparkling blue water that welcomed us. Louis ran into the water and began thrashing around trying to get his arms and legs to work together. It did not take him long.

"Edward, so hurry and learn to swim again. Test your strength. The water is just perfect warm and feels good. I think I am stronger but you see if you think you are and then we can have a race."

I splashed about trying to keep my balance while awkwardly walking into the water. It felt cold to me. Louis continued to urge me to swim and test my strength. I knew he was doing amazingly well when he got his swimming stroke rhythm so quickly. He had not been swimming since last season and considering he had been 'not with them' for more than a month his strength was excellent. I had to swim to warm up.

"Louis, does the salt water hurt you?" I asked as we came together standing face to face in several feet of water.

"No this water does not hurt me. So I feel something, maybe a tingle, but I imagine it feels good. Then I think I am ready for a race."

I felt up for the challenge but thought he was the stronger man. Perhaps he had an unfair advantage, but Louis suggested the race first. "Where shall we swim to? Any style? Any rules?" I asked.

"So what do you mean - style, Edward?"

"That means is there any special way we should race. Swim on our sides, or our backs, a butterfly stroke, or whatever."

Louis looked confused; "I have heard nothing of styles, only swimming. So I guess that means any style, no rules. See that rock," Louis pointed to a conspicuous rock at the far edge of the curving beach. "Let us swim to that."

With that he splashed off toward the rock and I, ignoring this uneven start, followed. In normal times I knew Louis would have the greater strength. He was physically larger, and therefore presumably stronger. I satisfied myself with the thought that these were not normal times. I would beat Louis.

We both stood by the rock at the same time. Neither of us entirely whole or healthy. It was a tie. When we walked out to rest on the shore, I asked the question I waited so patiently to ask. "Louis, what was your crime? Why were you in solitary?"

Louis played with the shells he had found. He switched them from hand to hand. He looked up with a quizzical expression I didn't understand. "What have you heard?" he asked.

"Father Mary introduced me to the two men who found you. They were Victor Emmanuel Saint-Aude, a farmer, and Elius Nelcha, a shoemaker. They were both strong, young men. I noticed that even though one was a shoemaker, both were barefoot, like most natives.

"I asked them 'Please tell me how you found the prisoner.' The shoemaker was the spokesman, probably from having more conversations with people than the farmer, who remained silent.

"The cobbler said they were in St. Pierre from Morne Rouge looking for objects left in the ruins. They did not think they would find anyone alive because they knew everyone in the city was dead. They knew this because they helped burn the bodies for days and found no living person. They did not expect to find anything at all because so many had gone through the ruins before.

"When they heard sounds near the jail, they didn't believe them. They asked each other, 'Did you hear something?' and then they agreed 'Yes.' Then they wanted to know if it was something playing a trick on them. Since they both heard the sounds, they decided to try to follow the noise. This was four days after the eruption and the ashes were still hot, but how could they resist finding out about what they heard?

"They didn't understand where the noise could be from. Maybe it was a spirit. They didn't know, but they followed the noise until they could tell someone was calling. The voice said, 'mister, mister, please help me. For God's sake help me. Come and help this poor prisoner.' So they knew it was a person and not a spirit, and he was in prison.

"They started to move things around to find the voice and at last they did find you alive in your cell. You had water, but no food. They fed you some soft fruit and helped you walk to Morne Rouge.

"Sometimes they tried to carry you between them, but that was difficult. You were so badly burned; they didn't know where to hold you. Sometimes they made a bridge with their hands and had you lie across their hands and they walked that way.

"They couldn't do that for long because the sun would begin to hurt the burns on your back and it was awkward to carry you that way. They did not think you would live to see Morne Rouge. It took all day to get there.

"I asked them to describe the cell for me. They said it was a solitary cell in the city prison. It had an opening, like a grate in the door and no windows.

"I asked if they knew of any other survivors. They thought you were the only one, but since then I heard of more. I think I told you. There was one woman found alive in a basement. She died a few hours after they took her out. One man taken to Carbet was quite mad. No one knew anything about him.

"The two men did not know you. Father Mary told them you were from Precheur, just like they were, but they swore they didn't know you.

"I asked if they knew why you were in jail. They repeated that you were in the solitary cell and the only people put in such a cell are the bad ones. They guessed you must be the murderer that killed a white soldier. They didn't know who else you might be. They didn't know for sure that you were the murderer, but they didn't think you were in solitary for spreading gossip in the marketplace. They said innocent men do not go in such cells.

"I asked if I was in any danger if I transported you to Fort-de-France. They said, 'He smells very bad from the burns. Only his smell is strong enough to hurt you, unless he has other powers.'

"I asked them, what other powers? They said, 'He survived and no one else survived like he did. He must have some strong powers."

Louis threw back his head in an explosion of laughter. "I have strong powers and I am a murderer. A murderer with strong powers. Is that the story you would like to tell your readers?" Louis asked in a teasing voice. "Is it more exciting to read that the survivor is a powerful murderer condemned to die? Maybe I was waiting for them to hang me? When I stood on tiptoe in my cell I could see them building the scaffold. It was such a vile murder that they put me immediately into a cell by myself. This is a good story. Is this what you want to hear?" Louis laughed and slapped the ground at the idea.

"Is it true?" I asked quite seriously.

"It is not true, but how will you ever find out the truth if I do not tell you? No, my friend, I did not kill a white man." Louis continued playing with the shells. I found the repetitive movement annoying.

"Are you going to tell me what you did?" I demanded abruptly. I could show annoyance now that I knew my own life was not in danger.

"No. I will not tell you about that but I will tell you about my prison cell."

CHAPTER ELEVEN

Louis was very matter-of-fact. "I was in what is called solitary confinement, the place they keep one person all alone. It was a small room with no windows. The door was solid. Very heavy. There was a small opening in the top part of the door. It had bars over it. I could pull myself up by the bars and look out. I could see some light that way. The cell had very thick walls so you could not hear much. It had a narrow wood bed. It was hard to do nothing and talk to no one.

"You had only one small opening in the cell?" I was surprised that the prison Louis described was so solid.

Louis's slight smile and mater-of-fact delivery faded. He answered soberly, "Yes. It was light enough from my little opening. I thought it must be morning. I was waiting for breakfast when it grew very dark," Louis sighed, waited for a few moments, and then began again.

"You hear little in the dungeon. If you listen very hard, you may hear someone walking to your door with food, the steps on the stones.

This morning I heard a terrible noise. I could even hear screams. Everyone was screaming, even me.

"After a few minutes there was no noise, but hot air and fine ash came in like a dense fog through the small opening in the door. I could feel this fog burning me. I did not know what to do. I jumped in agony around the cell. I curled up to be small. I called for help just like the others, yet I did not want to breath the hot air. I did not hear anything else.

"The hot air did not last very long. I do not know how long exactly. Maybe fifteen minutes. I did not see any fire or smoke. The only smell was my own burning flesh."

"You didn't catch on fire?"

"No," answered Louis. "There was no flame. The heat burned my back, but did not scorch my shirt. You saw how badly burned I was. I could not do nothing but curl up in a ball and try to keep the smallest part of me against the heat.

"When the heat seemed to be less, I got some water to drink. It is strange, but the water in my cell was not hot, even though there had been so much heat in the room. That water was still cool." Louis shook his head is disbelief. "Do you understand? The water in this place so hot - like Father Mary talks about hell - this water in my prison cell was cool!" Louis fell silent.

The comparison to hell definitely caught my attention. What an anomaly to have cool water in this particular hell. I interrupted the silence reluctantly. "Did you know it was Mt. Pelee erupting?"

"No. I did not know nothing."

"How did you feel when you knew the city was destroyed? I asked.

"I did not understand what happened at first. I guessed what happened, but I did not understand it. As I went through the ruins with the men who found me I was numb with my own pain and I did not realize what was around me.

"Have you ever seen something, then thought about it over and over in your mind because you didn't believe it? Maybe thinking about it again and again would make it easier to believe. So, you keep thinking about it. I have been like this for most of the time since the eruption. Now I believe what I saw and I want someone to blame.

This is a happening of such size that it can only be God who is to blame." Louis fell silent.

I started to talk to fill in the silence that came between us. "It is all quite remarkable," I began quietly. "Do you remember anything else while you were in the cell? Didn't you smell something? Sulfur maybe?"

"No. I only smelled my own burning flesh."

"Did you feel like you were going to suffocate?" I asked.

"No. It was hot, but I could breathe. It didn't suffocate me. It was just not pleasant because the air was so hot. I was afraid breathing would hurt. The fear was as bad as the heat." Louis deliberately threw the shells he had found back into the waves one at a time.

I admired the black man sitting beside me. In spite of the obvious fresh burn scars; he was still a strong handsome man. He was poorly educated, but he was intelligent. He usually answered questions simply and quietly. His temperament appeared even, with lapses of irrational anger. He talked about liking parties, yet it didn't fit his personality. He appeared somber, but his recent experience would be enough to sober any man. Then again, he laughed and made jokes.

Louis studied me as I was studying him. After a long silence Louis said, "I admire you. You work with your head and not with your hands like I do. You are a wise man. Tell me, am I cursed or blessed?"

I drew back, startled. "I don't know, Louis. I would say blessed because you are still alive."

"Does that mean that God spared me because he has a plan for me?"

"Father Mary might believe that, but I don't," I answered. "I think a man must fill his hours usefully, but he does not need to devote them only to God. We need to work to eat and wear clothes and stay warm in the cold. You said we need to work to enjoy parties. I don't think we need to work constantly to save our immortal souls. I am not sure I have an immortal soul," I concluded.

"You are much more a nonbeliever than I am. I feel I have a soul. It is the part of me that is better than what goes out to fish. It thinks for me and decides for me. I am cursed because I have to live with memories of things as they were. These memories are haunting me. There is something else. The way lava buried the people, or burning the bodies to dispose of them, this is not right. This is not proper. You cannot say good-bye in such a way. Maybe because there was no proper burial, these people are not truly dead. Maybe people die only when we forget them."

"The memories will leave with time. You said something else, Louis. You said I work with my mind and not my hands and you admire that. It isn't important what a man uses for his work, his mind or his hands. What is important is that the work is productive, that something comes of it." I paused thinking to myself. I did believe what I had just said; yet that would mean that Louis, the fisherman, was my equal. Was there any way that this ignorant black man could be my equal?

Louis interrupted my thoughts saying, "That is what I am afraid of. I may not be productive. I am anxious because I may have another loss that I do not even know yet. You will be productive. You have only lost time from our accident. I gained healing from Marie, but I have lost everything else. And you have something else, you can keep within yourself."

"What does that mean?" I asked.

"You do not show your feelings, except when you first stood up naked in the morning." Louis smiled broadly at the memory of my embarrassment, then continued in a low serious voice. "You are in control of yourself. You do not show pain. You choose what you will say very carefully, and you don't say very much."

"Maybe I am shy."

"No. I do not believe that. You talk to people to write about them. That is not shy."

"Louis, I meant shy about my private life."

"Why shouldn't you be? It is your personal life. I have a part of myself that I keep for myself and do not show to other people. But the part I show to people, what purpose does that serve? Do I have an obligation to do good? To serve God by the part that I show?"

"Do you feel like you have an obligation?"

"I do not know what I feel. I feel empty. I do not understand why I am living when everyone else in the city is dead. What is my purpose in living?"

"That, my dear Louis, is the eternal question. What purpose does anyone have? How do we go about it? Where does it get us? I don't know. I have some ideas that fit in with the question, but they don't answer it."

"Tell me your ideas, Edward," invited Louis.

"We are all dying. These people the volcano killed just went all at once. I don't question my right to be alive when people around me die. Death is the natural course of ending life."

"This death was not natural, Edward." Louis shook his head sadly. "No. It was not natural at all. Why am I still alive? I think I deserved to die."

"It sounds like you are alive because you are lucky. I don't think that courage had anything to do with it. I don't think God had malice that day toward the people who died. I do not think that any man who lives decently deserves to die. What do you think?"

"It was not courage," agreed Louis. "I just kept on living. I guess you are right. It must be a matter of luck. Because I am lucky, do I have a duty to do anything special with my life? Father Mary said that God spared me to set an example with my life, to do His work."

I answered, "I do not know that God uses people for examples. Father Mary tells us that in the afterlife we will learn all the answers.

Here on earth, right now, luck is as good an answer as anything else. Even if people aren't lucky maybe they still have a duty to do something with their lives. I don't know. I guess that each of us needs to use any talents we have in the best way we can. We all have limits. We must recognize these limits, but do the most we can with the talents we have. Nothing is perfect, certainly not our lives. To have pleasure we have to have something to contrast with it and so we have pain or trouble. We can't withdraw from life. We must be active. If nothing else to provide our own food and shelter."

"After we take care of food and shelter, what then, Edward?" asked Louis.

"Maybe we need to continue working productively, to fill the hours usefully. We need to sustain life and protect it, not perfect it."

"Perhaps you are right, Edward, but what about the problems the devil puts in our paths?"

"Do you believe that, Louis? I don't. The obstacles in life are not devils, or from the devil. They are just obstacles."

Louis answered slowly, "I have never thought about what I believe. I just believed what people told me. I didn't know that I could believe them or not believe them. No one told me I had a choice. I guess I did not think for myself. Why has it taken me so long to realize this?" Louis looked at me with surprise written on his face.

Suddenly, he slapped me on the back and began laughing. "We are so different. You are the most intelligent man I have ever known and I am a simple man," he laughed, repeating the phrase again and again. His laugh was infectious. It caught me up in his mood. Soon both of us were laughing at ourselves.

When we became calm again, Louis said, "You told me I have no devils in my path. That my problems are only obstacles and not devils? I have great obstacles. I want a boat of my own and a comfortable life. I have little education. I have very little opportunity and I am poor. Besides, even if I do get my boat, I will probably lose it."

"Louis, we have established that you are a lucky man," I told him. "If you get a boat, you will not lose it. You will have done something to earn your boat and that will keep you from losing it. I guess what I am trying to say is that in some ways we all make our own luck. If you make your own luck to get your boat, making your own luck will not let you lose your boat."

"What about if a storm comes up and wrecks it? Is that luck? Is that God? Is that the devil?"

"I don't know," I confessed.

"What do you want from life, Edward?"

I looked out on the ocean. What did I want? I did not want a boat. I had material wealth, thanks to my parents and their parents. I did not want or need more things. What I might want was more vague. It was something I never quite understood, and yet I did have some ideas.

"I will be honest with you and tell you what I have never confided in anyone else. I want to be successful at my work. I want people to know my name because my writing is good. I want my writing respected and admired long after I am dead. Is that a stupid idea?"

"That is a good answer. It is not stupid. When I fish, I want to catch fish. I want to be successful at my work too. I will not forget the boat, but maybe the boat will come if I am successful at my work. If I am a good fisherman with my boat, people will remember me long after I am dead. I don't think I will ever get my boat though. I don't think I will be that successful and I am not that lucky."

"Not that lucky! You survived. That is luck, fate, good fortune, a miracle and a blessing. I will hear no more talk of your being unlucky. You have survived. You can be a hero. You can go beyond survival and build on life's challenges. This can make you stronger, tougher, more able. What more do you want from life?"

"I do not want something so grand as to be a hero. I want a boat." Louis laughed and slapped his knee. "I want a boat," he repeated. "Have you seen our little boats? They hold two or three men. They are wooden and painted gay bright colors. I would like a red boat." His smile faded. He grew serious again. "I admire you. You are separate from problems. You see them better. You do not get all involved and upset like I do. I think of the boat. You think of your whole life."

"I admire you, Louis, because you get involved with people. I admire your expression of feelings, your curiosity. I live my life very evenly. You say you like to party. You have mountains and valleys in your life, and you survive both very well."

After some thought Louis responded, "Perhaps my answer is to live trying to be like the ideal island person. One who people admire because he is generous, even if he is poor. He is religious but not unfair or bossy about what other people believe. He works hard and takes care of his family, friends, godchildren and relatives. Does this sound right to you, Edward?"

"It sounds perfect to me. I'm beginning to think that every person is unique and can never be replaced because of his uniqueness. Every man has a name, a family, and dreams that will die unfulfilled." I could not believe I was talking. I went on. I couldn't leave well enough alone.

"It surprises me to find that in many ways you and I are alike. The difference between us, in how we live, is important. It is the difference between the intellect, or the mind, and feeling. You, Louis, are better at feeling than I will ever let myself be."

Louis was sad when he spoke. "So let us go back for our food now. We will sleep and grow stronger, then tomorrow I will take you fishing." Louis got up and started walking back to the shack.

CHAPTER TWELVE

"Have you been fishing in a *gommier* before?" Louis asked obviously eager to be out on the inviting blue water.

I eyed the large canoe with suspicion. Staying on land was suddenly very inviting to me. I was aware of the white sand beach cooled by soft perfumed air whispering over it. The undulating palm trees offered inviting shade. How could anyone want to go out on the dark ocean when there was so much to stay on shore for?

"You want to take me out on the ocean in this?" I blurted out. "Is this the kind of boat you want?" I asked in disbelief.

"Yes, but this boat belongs to the plantation," answered Louis ruefully. "I wish I had this boat. We will only borrow it to go out to where we can catch some fish to eat. So you look like you could use this boat you are dressed perfect for using it." Louis gestured at my garb, the native costume, white pants, white shirt and a large straw hat. "What is the problem?" He was smiling at me.

I swallowed hard. "I've never been on the ocean in something like this, or even a calm, placid, smooth lake for that matter."

164

"I will row us out. It also has a sail, but I don't think we need that. I want you to tell me about the sailors. You said some sailors in the harbor survived. I think that means I am not the only survivor as you say."

"You are the only survivor on land," I said with a sigh as I reluctantly helped Louis push the boat out into the water. "I'm not sure I want to do this," and I unwillingly climbed into the shell.

"It will be fun and we will find some good fish to eat. We will have good air to breath. We will feel better and better. When we get back we will be tired and get good sleep. So there are many advantages to fishing. Now tell me about the sailors."

I wasn't sure I could talk because the waves were making me feel sick, then we broke through the surf and the calmer rocking motion offered me hope I would survive this fishing trip.

"I went to the hospital in Fort-de-France," I began. "The nurse asked if I was sure I wanted to see them and she pinched her nose shut. When I assured her I did, she pointed to a ward down the hall. It was a dark antiseptic smelling hall, gray with age. It looked like no one cared for it."

Louis laughed. "That is why we don't go to hospital unless we are taken. We can take care of most things ourselves. Please to continue."

"When I opened the door, I saw the sailors were in all in one ward. The room was poorly lit and even the twenty beds, all with bright white sheets, didn't brighten the gray room. It smelled like sulfur and boric acid, and burned meat.

"There were about a dozen miserable looking men. None as bad as you and remember the eruption was about two weeks past before I saw them. Many had bandages on their hands or arms. About half the men were bandaged on the entire upper body and a few had their faces wrapped. I saw no eyebrows on any man."

"I wonder why that was? I have my eyebrows."

"Yes, and a good part of your body besides your face is unmarked, but they encountered more than heat."

"Please to go on, Edward. I will try not to interrupt."

"At first I heard only murmurs from them. No boisterous joking or noisy comments on any news they heard. The men were subdued. Probably morphine for the their pain.

"They turned to look at me as I walked into the ward. Of course they didn't recognize me. I wasn't a physician they knew and they didn't get visitors. They were suspicious. I wondered how to approach them. I felt their eyes on me so I knew I had their attention already. The question was how to get them to talk?

"I introduced myself, said I worked for a newspaper in Boston and the editor of the local newspaper told me that they were the survivors of the steamer *Roraima*. I said I'd like to talk to them about their experiences. I asked if they could tell me what happened to them at St. Pierre.

"The men were completely silent at first and I wondered if I had the wrong ward, but the smell and bandages convinced me it was the right one. I had to coax them a bit.

"After a short time, one man started to talk. He was very soft spoken and he appeared the most able to talk, the least burned. The others seemed happy to have him talk.

"He said they were from the passenger steamship the U. S. *Roraima*. Their shipmates, those not so badly burned, were sent back to New York. They could tell me about their experiences, but it wouldn't be big news because their shipmates back in the states already told their stories.

"I had to convince them I wanted to know their stories. It was important to what I was doing, my series of in-depth feature stories about the eruption. What they could tell me might be just what I needed to tip the scales in favor of an award."

"So that is why you want to know about me. You want to win an award. What kind of an award is this you want to win, Edward?"

"It's an acknowledgment of my skill as a writer. It says I am good at what I do. In fact, it says I'm the best. I have won several because I am the best and I want to show I am still the best. I wanted emotional stories and they should certainly be able to provide them."

"Is this why you want to write about me?"

"Yes, Louis. You are the only survivor, on land, and you were in prison, though you won't tell me why. Your story should win a prize for me, except, perhaps, too much time is passing and the story will be old, unless you were in prison for murder."

"Soon I will tell you," laughed Louis. "But now I am going to fish." He threw a fishing line set up with a line of hooks and weighted with a grooved stone. "I am going to catch us some poissons rouges, the finest red fish of the first quality." He held his hand to the line. When he saw the look on Edward's face he said, "I am listening to the line."

"What do you mean, listening?"

"To tell when I have some fish. Please to continue."

"I asked the sailors to start with their arrival at St. Pierre. The man answered with a stronger voice. He said they pulled into the harbor at St. Pierre about 6:15 in the morning, about one and a half hours before the eruption. When they dropped anchor, their decks were gray with ash. The *Roddam*, another passenger steamship pulled in soon after them.

"They counted eighteen ships in the harbor. Sixteen disappeared during the eruption. They survived, but the nurses told them their ship was completely destroyed. It burned until it burned itself out.

"He said twenty-eight shipmates died fighting the fires. Only two of the passengers survived. They didn't know what happened to the *Roddam*, the ship that pulled in just after them, so I told them the *Roddam* escaped. The badly burned Captain, Captain Freeman, managed to bring the ship in to the port of Castries on St. Lucia. He was the first to tell about the destruction of St. Pierre. According to his newspaper account, the *Roddam* still had steam up, so she managed to flounder away from the eruption. Every man on the deck died when 'the cloud', as the captain called it, struck the ship.

"When the ship arrived in Castries, it needed help getting into port. The ship had 50 tons of ash on her decks and only ten surviving crew members. Molten lava killed most of the crew. The captain told the people who helped bring them in, 'We come from hell'.

Louis gasped. "They were right. The heat was like hell. I don't know hell, but the priests who do say it is very very hot."

I paused for a moment before continuing. I felt like laughing at Louis who was giving priests credit for knowing hell personally, but I did have more to say.

"The chief officer of the *Roraima* introduced himself to me. His name was Ellery Scott. He said they thought the *Roddam* was coming to save them because about half past eight, the darkness that had descended on them lifted a little and they could see the other ship steaming toward them.

"When the ship was about one hundred feet away, she stopped and they thought maybe she hadn't seen them after all, so they sent up signal flares. The flares worked well. They burned brightly like fire works. With this signal the other ship had to know someone was alive on their ship, but the *Roddam* backed off into the darkness and didn't come back. They were glad to hear that if she couldn't save them, at least she saved some of her own crew.

"They were very curious about what I knew. No one had told them anything. So I told them about the French ship, *Suchet*. The one that picked them up and about thirty others as well. Most of the people they picked up did not live more than a few hours. They picked up three Italians off an overturned deck house. They also found their captain. He was alive when they found him, but died shortly after they got him out of the water."

"That ship's carpenter said he saw the captain on the ship and it was a miracle he lived at all. He was so badly burned, the crew couldn't recognize him. He had no face.

"Their captain tried to direct two of them so they could get at one of the lifeboats but it was impossible. It was so jammed in that twenty men couldn't budge it. Then he told them to jump overboard and save themselves. They thought they might still help some of the passengers, so they wouldn't jump.

"The sailors reported they went to find the captain later. When they got back to the bridge, he was gone. They thought he must have jumped or fallen overboard. They said his suffering must have been terrible because his face had burned off."

"Sweet Jesus," murmured Louis. "My face is not burned off. I am in a better way than I thought I was." He turned his attention to the fishing line. "That was a fair fish. A second has escaped." He hauled in the line missing two pieces of bait, rebaited the hooks and lowered the line into the water again. "Please to continue, Edward."

"You felt that fish?"

"Yes, I told you I was listening to the line. Please to continue."

"I asked them to tell me what kind of a day it was the day of the eruption. They said it was clear. Then before eight they heard four deafening explosions, like canon going off and there were two clouds over the volcano.

"The first cloud was immense and black and streaked with lightning. The second was a lighter gray with glowing red lines. This one came down the slope rapidly, following the line of the Roxelane River. With the clouds, there was a pulsating, throbbing roar. They said it sounded like a Gattling gun. Are you sure you didn't hear anything, Louis?"

"No. I did not hear anything but my own screams. I told you that before. So please to go on."

"They said the cloud that came along the river clutched the ground. Whatever that cloud touched burst into flames. Thousands of barrels of rum on the quay exploded and that explosion was incredible to them. I could never imagine that blast.

"They said the details, like what time it was, you don't know or care. You get caught up in trying to survive and you don't even know how much time has past. They didn't know anything about the time. They said it might have been minutes, it might have been hours. They did know for sure that the cloud burned everything in its path.

"I told them the official time was 7:50 a.m. because that is when the telegraph communications stopped. The reports said a few minutes later a mushroom shaped black cloud formed over Pelee. People reported it was traveling six or seven miles a minute. You can't see St. Pierre from Fort-de-France because of the mountains, but people here saw the cloud.

"In Carbet, the village to the south, they reported a twenty foot high wave half a mile wide that went at least three hundred feet along the coast. That wave came less than twenty minutes after the explosion."

"What about the people of Carbet?" asked Louis.

"Reports I've read said that people on the fringe of the village were very badly burned. Many died. I know the steamer *Esk* from Carbet reported ash covered it at five miles out. They saw only flames on shore. At eight miles out the ship still felt heat from hot stones and ashes on her deck. She escaped with difficulty.

"The sailors asked about St. Pierre, if there was anything left. I answered carefully because I was surprised at how little they knew. I told them the city burned for days. The acting governor sent the *Suchet* to check the city. Their first look through the binoculars didn't show a living thing. It was too hot to land.

"Finally, the Captain of the Suchet could land. He was the first, after the eruption. He said there was not a single tree standing. Dead bodies littered the ground. Yet, the fountain in Place Bertin, where he came ashore, was still flowing with clear, cool water. No one in the city survived the eruption. The sailors were shocked.

"They had heard about a memorial service in Paris. They didn't know the service was for an entire city."

Louis interrupted, "It is good that there was such a service. They didn't get a proper burial. It is good someone prayed for them. Maybe there souls can rest if enough pray for them."

"There was a memorial service in London and Rome also," I offered. After a suitable pause allowing us each a moment of remembrance I continued, "I asked them to tell me more about the cloud that came down on them. The captain answered me. He said the darkness was something appalling. You could see only the glow of flames through the falling ashes. Another man interrupted him saying he was in the engine room and he couldn't even see the man working with him who was standing two feet away.

"The captain continued by saying the ship took fire in several places from hot ashes falling. He said the ashes fell quite thickly at first. This ash was so hot it burned material on contact. Then the ship listed to starboard and pointed to the shore.

"He told me small, sizzling stones, came like a falling rain after the ash. The stones hissed when they hit the water. The sailors might have had some protection at first, from all the ash that fell, but then came a hot mud.

"Fires were starting up all over the ship, then this thick hot mud came raining down. It was like cement. It coated everything like glue. The captain pulled a tarp over his head. He said that helped. He still had to clean off his face every few seconds to see anything. It was not exactly burning, but it steamed.

"The captain told me about another sailor, he thought it was the assistant purser, who stood beside him. The other man's head was weighed down with the mud. He begged the captain to break it off his head, but the captain was afraid he would scalp him when he took the mud off his head. But it did break off. The man's whole scalp must have been badly scorched. The captain could feel the heat himself and thought it must have baked the top of the other man's head, but he couldn't tell because the man still had hair.

"Another sailor told me the story of the captain of the Italian bark, *Orsolino*. They were sailing with sugar for Le Havre. The ship was only half full and authorities would not issue clearing papers to him. The shippers said they would have him arrested in Le Havre unless he went out with a full load. Two customs officers went out to stop the ship from sailing and he told them they were welcome to come with him to France, but he was not staying. The officers went back to St. Pierre and he sailed. He survived and I'll bet they didn't arrest him in France either.

"Louis, did you smell anything?"

"Just my own burning flesh."

"I asked the sailors if they smelled anything and they said they didn't want to smell anything because they didn't want to breathe hot air."

"That is true, Edward. I tried to breathe as little as possible because I didn't want to burn my lungs. I guess if there was a smell I noticed, it was sulfur, sulfur and ash." Louis leaned forward with anticipation. "I have two fish, but the shark is going to eat one."

I looked out over the water with apprehension and saw the tail of the shark swimming away from us. I watched with admiration as Louis pulled in one large fish and a small part of another. The shark got almost all of it.

Louis turned to me. "You row back and I will tell you what my crime was."

CHAPTER THIRTEEN

My arms started aching just seeing the distance I had to row to get back to shore. When I focused my eyes closer to the little boat, I saw the dark flash of a fast moving large fish. 'Sharks' I muttered to myself and we were only inches from water in an ungainly dugout.

"Louis, could you start talking? I admire the color of the water, the warm air and the calm rocking motion, but this boat of yours, this canoe, is making me nervous and I think there is a shark or two following us."

"You are so comical for an educated man," Louis laughed. "Besides it is only one little shark." He leaned his head toward his chest a little and flashed a sideways grin at me. "So I talk for the snake and I talk for the shark and the deep water." He laughed again.

"I guess you can laugh at me," I replied. "I'll have to admit I'm something of a coward." I felt foolish admitting this weakness to Louis.

"So I will talk to help you and I will tell you my crime, then you can help me with my problem. You have been very good to help me

179

understand what happened to my people and my city. I think you have been very honest with me and I know you do want to know my crime so you can write about it and get a lot of notice, fame or reputation or some such thing.

"So I will tell you my problem when I am finished telling you my crime. It is a very small crime and I surely believe you will be disappointed with me." Louis tried to look apologetic, but his sad face was lost on me. I was pretending to look intently at the shoreline, while concentrating on what I was about to hear. At last my prize-winning feature story.

This moment was what I had been waiting for, but I did not want to appear too eager. My arms suddenly grew stronger. My body leaned into the rowing with more intensity. Louis started talking and I kept time pulling on the oars.

Louis said, "While I was working in the city one day, I saw a friend. He told me that the preacher man was going to have a party. I know this preacher man. Now this preacher man is a good man and his parties are also good.

"So I work for this preacher man sometimes, but sometimes I work for a sailor or a farmer. It depends who has the work to do. But next, after I saw my friend, I saw this preacher man that I sometimes work for. He said he was going to have a big party and he wanted me to come because he knows I like parties and if I am there at the party everyone has fun. So that is why he wanted me."

"Is he a priest?" I asked.

"No. A preacher man. He is one of us that talks about things at meetings. Maybe he knows a little more than we do because he reads easily and understands quickly. He thinks he knows more, but he is still a good man. You remind me of him. You are educated but you are afraid of snakes and sharks. I don't think he is afraid of snakes, but you remind me of him. So he calls himself a preacher. We have several preachers around. He is not a priest."

"Okay, he is not a priest, he is a preacher. Go on with your story." I urged him a little sharply, my impatience showing. My focus, my need to know Louis' crime was primary and the story was not moving quickly enough now that Louis was finally talking.

"So the interruption was yours," countered Louis, who smiled at Edward, but remained quiet. I did not rise to the bait. I was impatient, but Louis wouldn't get me to show my impatience again so soon.

Finally Louis cleared his throat and started talking. "So I went to this preacher man's party. It was a good party just like he promised. It was so wonderful good I was away all night and went back far too late in the morning. If I went back earlier, they would not have noticed I was gone. They noticed because I was away all night. I made people mad because I was not being serious about prison. So I was put in the dungeon for eight days, an example of what not to do."

I stopped rowing momentarily, dragging the oars listlessly in the water. "Let me get this straight. You were released from the prison to do outside work because it was a minor crime you committed. You went to a party and didn't come back to the prison until very late in the morning. Is that right so far?"

"Yes." Louis nodded.

"The prison officials wanted to make an example of you so they put you in solitary with an eight day sentence."

"Yes." Louis nodded again.

"Okay. That tells me why you were in solitary. It doesn't tell me what your crime was to get you in prison in the first place. I know they don't let murderers out to work, so I guess I have to give that idea up."

I started rowing again. Whatever the crime Louis committed, I had the sinking feeling I didn't have the story I wanted. Reluctantly I asked, "So tell me what did you do? What was this little crime of yours that was big enough to land you in prison?" I bit my lip, wanting to hear the answer but afraid of disappointment at learning what the crime was.

Louis rubbed his hands together and looked around trying to delay his answer. First he looked up and down, then from side to side. When I caught his wandering gaze Louis mumbled, "You will laugh at me. My crime is not so important as you want it to be."

"No, I won't laugh at you," I promised with a sigh. "Come on. Tell me."

Reluctantly Louis started to talk again. "So I got drunk and got in a fight at a party. I wounded a friend with a cutlass. I cut him. It was a very small cut. He almost did not bleed at all. In a way it was his

183

fault. He was drunk too or I could not have hit him. He is usually too quick.

"They arrested me. Not because my friend insisted, he did not, but other people thought I was a danger and needed punishment. So there was nothing to deny because I did cut him. They sentenced me to one month in prison. They released me during the day for work around the city. So it was very boring."

"That's all!" My voice boomed across the water. I did not know whether to laugh or feel rage at being cheated out of a good story. I took a deep breath while I regained control of his outrage at Louis' small crime. In a way it was funny. A murderer who wasn't. Then I said calmly, "Solitary confinement for breaking a curfew of some kind? There is no story here. You just like to party and you broke curfew because you like to party. That landed you in solitary and the thick walls, or whatever, saved your life. This is disappointing to me." I was plainly frustrated.

Louis was contrite. "So for your story you can say I was a murderer. That is a better story isn't it?" he offered lamely. "No one will know. You can say anything."

"No, it isn't a better story if you are a murderer—Yes, it is a better story. Just think of it, the only survivor is a condemned murderer. But I have to be honest. I am not writing fiction. I want to write about the survivor, about you. Your story, just the fact of your survival, is probably interesting to someone, though I must admit it's not as interesting to me."

"So do you see why I need to know everything that happened?" asked Louis meekly. "I must know where I fit this puzzle. I am not worthy to survive. You would say even my crime is not worthy. My question is still the same, should I go on living or should I kill myself, being such an unworthy person?"

After a pause I answered him. "It seems very obvious to me that the other natives think you are special. The way they treat you, they expect you to go on living."

"So, Edward, you know they are superstitious. They think because I survived I am somehow like God that I am special and you know I am not special." Louis shook his head sadly. "I am not special," he muttered listlessly.

The silence settled uncomfortably on my shoulders. I did not know what to say.

"So, Edward, you know that everyone else will return to what is usual for them, but my whole life is around me in bits. I am like a puzzle with many pieces but the puzzle cannot ever fit together because there are pieces missing. You must help me, Edward. You must tell me what my life means."

I quietly chuckled to myself. "Louis, I may know a great deal, I may be arrogant, but I am not conceited enough to assume I know the meaning of any life. Not yours. Not even my own.

"We, somewhat educated people, believe the earth goes on forever, that time is endless. Everything is here because we perceive it to be here. If I spend too long considering what the endless universe means, or what man's place in it means, I'll go mad. So I don't think about it, and here you are, asking me if you should take your life or not. You are asking me the importance of your life in the world. For myself, I say we don't know who God is, or what life is all about. Maybe this is a question for Father Mary."

"So he says I am here to do God's work and we know that is not so." Louis looked away, vacantly surveying the shoreline we were fast approaching. A moving figure on the beach caught his eye and he pointed it out to me.

"Do you see that woman?" Louis nodded his head toward the beach. I saw a small bent blue wrapped figure moving quickly away from the beach into the palm trees, toward the cottage. "That is our future," said Louis quietly. "So maybe she has my answer. She is the wise woman and she is very powerful. She is more powerful than Marie. She can help anyone she chooses, because she knows everything. I have only heard about her, but I never saw her before. It is a great honor to meet her, an even greater honor if she talks to me. I hope she will help me."

Louis jumped out of the boat into the water and started pulling the boat onto the sand.

"Maybe this will be a good story yet," I muttered as I jumped over the edge of the boat. I lost my footing in the water and came down with a splash; face first, my straw hat floating away.

Louis laughed when he heard me muttering then falling flat. "So what will make a good story? That you cannot walk after you are on the water for some little time? Maybe that is a good story?"

"I don't see what's so funny." I grabbed my hat and shook myself.

"So you do not see anything funny here?"

"No. I don't."

"So, okay. There is nothing funny," said Louis with a broad smile. "So what will make a good story?"

"What the woman tells you."

"Tells us," corrected Louis. "If you have your legs to walk on land, we can go back now."

"No, I don't have my land legs back yet. Let me move around a little and dry out a bit." I took my clothes off and rung them out.

"So you should spread them out and let them dry," suggested Louis.

"Good idea." I spread his clothes out. "I guess I can take the sun."

"No, go back in the shade. Parts of you are too white and the sun will make your skin all red. There is no burn good for the body."

Louis pulled me by his arm toward the palm trees. The cool shade was welcome.

I began pacing back and forth and finally my legs felt firmly planted on the ground. "I think I am going to be able to walk like a normal person again after all."

Louis said, "So of course. You will get better and better at going out to sea. You need only some practice. You may even be a fisherman someday." He slapped my thigh with laughter. To him it was an amusing thought.

I turned away and went to get my clothes. They were still a little damp, but I put them on anyway. I did not appreciate Louis' attempts at humor at my expense.

Louis followed me contritely. "So maybe this is not funny. You are not meant to be a fisherman anyway."

"No, I don't think I am meant to be a fisherman, but if I don't come up with an exciting story I may have to learn how to fish for a living. Your problem is bigger than mine, but this time away from work may cost me my job."

"Do you think it is as serious as all that?"

"No, probably not as serious as that, but it will take some time and effort to regain my position in terms of prestige."

"So what is this prestige? I do not know this word."

"Prestige is how highly other people value you. What your reputation is," I told him.

This gave Louis something to think about. After a time he said, "When I bring good fish in to eat and everyone says how very excellent the red fish is, then I have prestige?"

"Yes, I suppose so."

"But to keep this prestige I must always bring in such good fish?" asked Louis.

"Yes."

"So Edward I see your problem. You must always write a good story. You can never stop or you lose something important to you. So I am very sorry that my story is not good for you and you will lose your prestige. I will have to think of a good story. Maybe with the wise woman or with the healing ceremony. Not to worry Edward, I can help you think of some other story."

"I hope so. Maybe the wise woman will give me some earthshaking information."

"Maybe this will be so, but I do not understand why you want to shake the earth. So let us go and see if she is ready for us, but remember one thing, do not talk to her unless she asks you to talk." With that warning in my ears, I followed Louis back toward the hut.

CHAPTER FOURTEEN

The enormous black woman outside the shack said, "Now you be quiet and patient until the wise woman is ready for you. I don't want no noise to bother us while we're getting ready."

We men tried to wait quietly, but we both were eager to talk. I had many questions I wanted to ask Louis. I didn't want to sit quietly. Louis had the same idea and we cautiously leaned toward each other. I whispered, "What is there to prepare?"

"I don't know," Louis murmured back with a shrug.

"What is going to happen?" I whispered again.

"So I do not know. I have never been to the wise woman's counsels before. I have only heard most wondrous things about them. Everyone on the island has heard about this special woman. She is the number one seer on the island and she is very powerful."

"Louis, am I expected to do anything?"

"No. She does everything."

"Does the meeting involve any physical action? Any pain?"

"I've heard enough," said the large woman loudly as she stuck her head out of the doorway. "You show respect and stop that whispering. You hear me?"

We sat back in the chairs and stopped trying to communicate. I motioned with my hand to the forest area waving it and mouthing "let's go." Louis shook his head no.

I collapsed back to on my chair. I desperately wanted to know just what was going on but, unwillingly, I held my tongue. I was the outsider here. Whatever preparations were going on, they were serious and I was not the person to interrupt them.

Finally a woman motioned us to enter the shack. The room was dark. I didn't understand how the women managed to darken it. I was never aware of any curtains and I knew quite positively that the shack didn't have shutters strong enough to keep out even fragile moonlight. I wanted to learn how they darkened the room so completely, but my eyes did not adjust to the dark quickly enough to focus on any details.

Something sweet was hanging in the air like a fog or a mist. It was not incense. It did not have the aroma of the East about it. The odor was not the product of exotic flowers and plants I could recognize.

The only smell that entered my mind to identify the scent was the odor of orange marmalade, which made no sense. I decided I should not even try to connect with reality. The connections were confusing. I would absorb the surroundings and learn what I might. I could analyze what happened rationally later.

Someone was leading me toward the end of the room where the beds usually were. What happened to the beds? I could barely see a figure sitting on the floor against the wall. It didn't matter. As my eyes got used to the dark, I decided the figure must be that of the wise woman. I could see two statues with candles at their bases, one at each side of the seated figure. They looked like statutes of saints, but I did not recognize them. There was no doubt they were religious statutes. That much was certain.

Louis motioned for me to sit cross-legged on the floor beside him in front of the figure. Now I could tell it was the old woman.

She was wearing a head covering not typical of the natives, who usually wore turbans. She was wearing something resembling a draped veil, something that might have come out of the East, something exotic. In the dimness I could not identify a color, or where the fabric began or ended. I knew she was an old woman. I could not guess how old—eighty, ninety, ageless?

I felt I was entering a warm silent cave, not sitting with my legs crossed in a bare wood shack. There were many candles burning, yet the lighting was still dreadfully dim even when my eyes became accustomed to the dark. The candles flickered and cast only hints of shadows on the wall. One particular large candle drew my attention. It seemed to have multiple flames coming from one wick. It was hypnotic to watch.

Marie placed steaming cups of broth in front of us. "Sip slowly," she warned.

In the warm, aromatic calm of this cave I felt I was moving away from my body. I felt like a spirit. I tried to reconnect with reality, but the idea of floating free was more exciting. I felt that with some effort I could float to the ceiling and look down on my body. I could go outside and float over the trees. I simply decided to stay beside myself, near my own physical body and watch what happened. It was the easiest thing to do.

When the wise woman spoke, she had the usually beautiful, soothing, harmonious musical quality to her voice. She sounded incredibly young and gentle. She had the body of an old woman, but her voice was like an angel talking.

"One of my powers is to foretell happenings by using a person's colors. The aura. This will work well for both of you. I am getting strong shades. I will start with you, Louis Ciparis. First, I will surround you with your color for your protection, so only good will come from what I see for you."

The woman became very still. Her eyes were open, looking straight ahead and seeing nothing but Louis' eyes. Her body rocked slowly back and forth. I knew that time was passing, but I had no idea how much time. The woman sighed. A lifeless expression spread over her face. As her face relaxed from the forehead to the chin, there was a noticeable difference in her features. Her skin became smooth. She had no wrinkles left. Her face was suddenly young, like an eraser took away the lines.

"I see muted red with a tinge of muted orange for you, Louis Ciparis. These muted colors mean you are still in distress. They will become clear as you heal and find your place in the world again.

"There are two sides to your spirit. You are honest, but you have an explosive temper. You have been quick to act. You act too quickly sometimes. You have not always given thought to what you do. Always remember; never hold a grudge. The problem may lie in your own actions.

"This red, like fire, has tamed you so now you will be able to think carefully before you act. Remember, you have acted too quickly in the past and now that is not necessary. You have time. Always remember, you do have time.

"The big need of your life is to find your purpose again. You must ask yourself questions about who you are. Then answer—I am—My job is to—I do—You will know your purpose then. Remember most people don't know what they want in life. You should answer these questions then remember your answers. Then you will know what you want to have, what you want to do, what you want to be.

"This is a big job. It will take time. You must work at it every day. Do not block yourself. Go to your purpose a little at a time. It does not make a difference how much you get done, just that you do some little thing each day to keep you moving. You will always be going forward."

The air was thick and heavy, enveloping everything and weighing down our lungs. When she stopped talking everyone's breathing came easier. When the woman spoke again, she started from exactly where she had left off, as though no time had passed, but an eternity had passed.

"You are very demanding of yourself, Louis. Do not expect more of yourself than you expect of another man. Be kind to yourself. You have a new body that will serve you well. You will enjoy life again. Do not judge yourself by bad tempered rules. You give your finest effort and people will judge you by that. Do not believe that other people disapprove of you. Making large demands on yourself will only worry you and make you unhappy. It is not necessary. Keep this in mind. Do you understand?" Louis slowly, almost imperceptibly, nodded yes.

"You need to find a woman in a quiet place. You will not find her at a party. If you do not find her, do not worry. She will find you. She is steady and kind. She will support you, in your work and in your thinking, even when you do not ask for help. You may move slowly in this relationship, but she will not reject you. Remember this.

"Louis, you would like to live in a world of beauty and quiet with people who are always gentle. I see a large boat. You will go away from here on a boat. The place you go to will not be the beautiful world you want. You will not find that beautiful world as you travel. When you come back, you create your own world. You may be like a turtle and pull your body inside the shell for a while. You will be safe hiding in yourself, but you must not be distant when you return here to make your home again. Do you understand?"

Ciparis shook his head "no." This he did not understand. The woman went on, ignoring him. He did not say anything.

"Just remember what I tell you. You will understand soon. Today the important thing is for you to begin to bring order back into your life. This will give you control. You are not helpless. Things will go wrong, but these are not problems like a mountain that never grows smaller. Do not strive for money. It does not offer anything of value to you once you have your boat.

"It is good for you to work alone. You should not work with many people. It will bring you unhappiness once you have what you want.

"You must not worry. There is no reason to worry. You feel poor because you have little teaching. You think you have no chance for good things to happen. Do not feel this way. I see a comfortable orderly life. You gain much if you work at achieving success in small things.

"I see a chance that gives you the boat you want. You fear getting what you want then losing it. This is not what will happen to you. You are safe in the world of nature. The elements will be kind to you.

"Be cheerful in your labor. Work with things you can see, feel, hear, taste and smell. I see color and excitement for you. You enjoy this, but it is hard for you and makes you tired when people stare at you. Then there will be calm. You must take the risk to get what you want. I promise you will not lose the boat once you have it. Do you understand? What do you want to ask me?" The woman became old again.

"What is this risk?" asked Louis.

"I cannot see what it is. It is something you have never done before. You must do it. It may seem wrong or strange, but you must do this new thing before you get your wish. There is no other way."

"Where does the big boat go?"

"Away from here, but you do come back. I do not see where you go on this boat. It is not your boat. I do see that future years are kind to you."

"Do you see when I die?"

"I did not see that. Are you worried because your burns may have weakened you so you will die soon?"

"Yes."

"You will live to be an old man. Do not feel that what has happened to you has marked you forever. You have been through a fearful devastation. It has been painful and deforming and you question if you are the same person you were before. You are the same in your spirit - your soul - but there are changes in what you will show to the world. Your body has changed. It looks different. It is not as strong. People will respond to you in a different way. You are still recovering, not just your body, but your spirit. Be patient with yourself. Be kind to yourself. Give yourself time to learn. Do you understand?" Louis nodded yes.

"But why did this happen to me? Why am I alive?"

"I do not know. I cannot give you an answer that never changes. A wiser person can help you find an answer, but you must learn this for yourself. We all know that every happening has a life of its own. There are no accidents for the true believer. Remember life is a gift. Perhaps this is to make you a better person."

"Do I owe a debt to the dead?"

"Only to live a good life. To show them respect by living the best life you can. The life that they would have wanted had they lived. You must have the courage to survive when all is lost. To take your own life when you have lost everything is the easy way out for you. You do have a debt of a kind to those who died. Your debt is to stay alive with dignity and decency. Do you understand?" Louis nodded yes.

"I must rest," she said. "Then I will see the other man clearly. He does not believe, but he will. Leave me for a while."

As we left the shack, the brilliant sun assaulted our eyes. Blinded, we staggered to the chairs to sit down. We rubbed our eyes and took in deep breaths of fresh air. The air was cool and smelled of sweet orchids. With each fresh breath we took in, we were able to relax our eyes. From a clenched hard squint to fully opened, our eyes were like flowers blooming, opening to the splendid greens and yellows around us.

Louis spoke with nervous agitation. "You must believe now. You see how she is correct. She has never met me, but she knows all about me. My dreams. My faults. She has exposed me. You must believe."

"Maybe I am a little less skeptical, but I don't believe her. She does give quite a good performance. She is intelligent. She puts us in a comfortable situation where we relax and even want to fall asleep. Then when we are stupid with the warm air and whatever fragrance she is hypnotizing us with, she says anything and we believe her.

"She has heard rumors. She knows you were a fisherman, so of course you want a boat. She knows all men have common faults. She has categories of people and she fits us in to the slots."

"Edward, your turn is coming. We will see what you say when she exposes you for what you are," Louis snarled. He turned away from me.

"I see you believe her, but your disposition has not improved yet." I had the last word before the door opened and the woman beckoned them to come in. I approached the shack with some reluctance.

CHAPTER FIFTEEN

The old woman turned her attention to me. She fixed her eyes on my eyes and by looking back at her, I was imprisoned. I could not look away. I could not hear any sound but the sound of her voice. I could not feel my own body, only a space filled with tension.

"Now I will see your color." Her calm, unlined face showed her trance was in effect again. "I will clothe you in your own color to protect you from harm." She paused and I felt the effect of her concentrated gaze.

"I see green for you, Edward. It is a harsh green and needs to become softer. That I see green is quite correct, there are many people with green for the things they create, but this is a cold heartless green. It has no feeling, no warmth. Green does not need to be so cold.

"It is this way because you keep it so. You keep yourself in an emotional box and do not give yourself any way to move out of this place you keep yourself closed up in. This is a choice you have. You can make the green a soft one that feeds other people and yourself as well.

"Your biggest enemy is patterns you repeat that make you a meaningless speck in the world. You, too, must move toward a purpose. You are not a watcher. You must do things to be satisfied. Interesting labor is one of the true possessions of a good life. This can be yours. One way to this path is to serve others. You also serve yourself when you serve others. Remember, you also serve yourself when you serve others. This is primary to your life.

"I can see that you move deliberately and speak no more than necessary to get the information you want. You are solid and steady and nothing disturbs your tranquility as long as you can reason in your head.

"You want to be left alone. You do not like groups of other people around you. For a person who works talking to people this is not good. This makes your green sharp. You must overcome this.

"I can see you are stubborn once you have made your mind up, but you are slow to take an action, and that is good. You are practical, very deliberate and usually careful. This is all fitting but you are all in the head, Edward, and this is part of your problem. Your response to the challenges of life is to think about them. You see life as a giant list of work to be finished. The major lesson for you to learn is that life can be easy and fun. You must give up your need to be perfect.

"You are productive and imaginative, but you fear that what you create and what you accomplish will not be good enough. That other people will find you lacking. This is not so.

"After you leave this island, a blonde woman from a ship will become your wife. To marry her and to make a home is very important to you. Your home is your shelter and helps to soften your green. Because of this woman you must not attend the bamboche tonight, or ever. It is not for you. When you marry her you must make other changes in your life. Your wife will be faithful to you and will give you all that you need, but you must ask her. Remember that.

"I see you at a desk working with paper. You are happy, but you do not talk to as many people as you have before. You are perfecting the work of other men.

"Do not think that people will not notice you. Your reputation is secure among those important to you. You do not need to think that you should, or must, have the approval of every man. Keep that in mind. You are special."

The old woman paused. Marie placed fresh bowls of steaming broth before us. As we sipped quietly, I went even deeper into the warmth and darkness enclosing me. There was no sound to disturb the peace of this place. Not even the sound of people breathing. The sound of life disappeared.

"Do not get ugly when you feel worried. Do not snarl at people. Stay as calm as you appear. You must find work that will keep you from worry, but do not make the mistake of giving your soul to that work. Do you understand?"

I did not understand, but I nodded my head that I did. I could not think of anything I would give my soul for. Yet, I could not interrupt the woman and I did not wish to hear my own voice. I was a dispassionate observer; I was rational in all areas of my life. I did not understand what was going on but I would think about it later, not now. It might mean something to me later in the reality of daylight.

"You must maintain order. This order will give you the control you want - to be first, to be a leader. Control is important to you. Remember what I am telling you.

"There is an obstacle. I see something rigid, hard and cold, but it changes. You think that you do not have feelings for other people. This is not true. You have buried these feelings. You can bring them to the surface and expose them to sunshine and air. The feelings are there. When you know yourself better, they will come out of the grave that you have made for them. Your feelings will become softer and warmer.

"You must stop viewing the world as something outside to be watched and commented on. You are in the world. You must teach yourself that life is good and it can be easy and fun.

"You are jealous of Louis. You think he has another chance to shape his life to be different from what might have been. You are wrong. We each of us have that chance every day. You can change your life. Do you understand?

"There is no risk for you. You think there is one, but it is in your mind. It is not real. Remember what I am telling you. What do you want to ask me?"

"If I marry and change my work, will I be happy?"

"You are happy now, if you permit yourself to be happy. You will be even more joyful if you make these changes. If you make these changes, you will not fear people seeing you as cold and without heart. You can become warmer and gentler without destroying your picture of yourself as a man who uses only his mind."

The woman went further into her trance. When she spoke again, her voice was so soft it was difficult to hear. Everyone strained to listen. The silence was complete except for the breathy remarks of the old woman with the young face.

"For both of you, I say choose the calling that suits you. Concentrate on that one and let others be. Do not envy what someone else has. Work hard. You can have what you want for yourself. You hold contentment in yourselves.

"Every day should be a festival. Not like a party, but like a celebration of life. You can't retire from life. You will not find contentment if you underestimate the world. You must be active.

"You have a duty to question what you believe. You must ask 'Why do I believe this?' Something positive comes from any circumstance. Do not look for the bad when the good is available."

There was a pause, a suspension of time. I did not know how long it was before the woman spoke again. "I have one last message for you. Louis and Edward, both of you hear me now; you are not to go to bamboche. It is not right for either of you. Do not refuse this. It is for your own well being. If you ignore this, you will regret it."

In the silence, the woman's face slowly turned old and wrinkled as time eased her back into the present. I became aware of the stillness pressing in on me. The scent and warmth of the room were suddenly all wrong. It was heavy. It was oppressive. I could not breathe. I needed fresh air and sunshine. How long had we been in this tomb? The more anxious I was to be outside, the brighter the room became. It was as if my uneasiness drew the sunlight and fresh air into the room through the open door. At last, people moved and talked freely.

I felt in control of my own body again as the sensation of floating disappeared. Louis and I both got up and stretched as the people around us left. The excessive warmth disappeared and the unusual smell with it. I could breathe freely.

Louis turned to me. "What will you do, Edward?"

"The wise woman says I'll find a wife going home on the ship and become an editor once I am back. I don't think this will happen. I don't think your seer is all that good. She may have an idea of what I am like, but the rest is just a guess."

"You are wrong, but that is not important. You will learn. So what is an editor?"

"He goes over other peoples work before the newspaper or magazine prints it. To be sure everything is in order."

"Edward, what you say is interesting, but it is not what I meant when I asked what you will do. I want to know what you will do the night of the bamboche? She said we were not to go. So will you try to go?"

"I don't know. Everyone else is going which leaves us by ourselves. I can understand why I can't go, but I don't understand why you can't."

"So I do not understand why both of us cannot go. Why do you say you can understand why you do not go but you do not understand why I cannot go? Why not? Maybe you do not want to go?"

"I would like to go. It would be quite a remarkable experience. A night of uninhibited drinking and love making would show I was ready to return to the outside world, though it might make me want to stay here.

"But I think I can't go because I'm a white man and not in any way related to this island or anything on it. I don't have any standing here. I'm an outsider. I'm a stranger. You do have standing. You are a voodoo mystery, so I certainly don't understand why they are keeping you away."

"Unhappily, neither do I. So I will talk to Marie for certain." As Louis stomped away I thought, Louis is not paying attention to the seer yet. His anger is not under control. Maybe the seer did know something after all.

I walked to a shady area and sat on a log under a palm tree. The seer told me my future and she also captured my personal essence. I was a passive, cold person. I had a lot to think about.

Louis came walking back toward the shack with a smile and jaunty walk, obviously pleased with himself. He caught sight of me and came to sit on the log beside me.

"Your spirits appear to be vastly improved. What did you find out?" I asked hoping there was still a chance for me to enjoy a night of unbridled passion.

"Happily Marie says we have the healing ceremony tonight and we should see how that works first. If it is very good, it will be exciting news for us, more important than bamboche. If Marie is able, she will talk the wise woman into letting us attend bamboche. But you see they may not have one if the healing ceremony is a very good one. So there may be nothing to talk the wise woman into. We may be able to leave for Fort-de-France tomorrow."

I was momentarily stunned. "You are happy about this? About going to Fort-de-France and not having *bamboche?*"

"So I think maybe I am happy. I do not think the wise woman will change her mind, so it is better not to have *bamboche* at all. Then I do not miss anything and I do not worry if my body is not pleasing to the woman, or if I have a problem to please her."

"I must say I'm disappointed, I guess the healing ceremony may be the only ritual I ever get to see."

"So you have never seen anything voodoo?" asked Louis. "I am surprised you have been on this island many times and have never seen the signs?"

I nodded my head negatively. "That's right, I haven't, except possibly once many years ago, when my family was visiting the Island, I saw part of a voodoo ritual that frightened me. I was very young. I believe it was a nighttime burial.

"There was a steady monotonous drumming. As a group of people drew closer, I heard the noise of sticks hitting together in different rhythms. Some were carrying torches and others were dancing wildly in the shadows they cast.

"No, maybe not dancing. They were twisting and slithering like snakes. They appeared to be going to the cemetery.

"I heard them chanting too. It sounded mournful. It was the sound of people lamenting their dead. It was eerie and I was frightened by it. My Negro nursemaid said there was nothing to fear. They were making houses for *duppys*, burying their dead in the manner of the culture.

"My parents weren't upset about me seeing the procession, except when it came closer and they saw that many were naked. They probably took off their clothes in the frenzy of chanting and drumming.

"We were too far from the cemetery to see just what happened next, but the atmosphere was euphoric and exciting. There was something magnetic about this group. If I had been with them, I could see myself whipping my clothes off and moving like a wild animal by torchlight.

"It was a typical warm Caribbean night and the scene was frightening, but it was also electrifying. You know, I can't remember if there were children in the group or not."

"So there probably were children in the group and I can tell you what you missed, Edward. Did you see animals in the group of people?"

"Yes, and a goat and two chickens."

"So when they reached the cemetery, those animals had their throats slashed and their blood drained. The voodoo priest or priestess drinks the warm blood. After the blood drinking, the singing, chanting and drum playing continues and the dancing grows even wilder than what you saw. On a party night, or *bamboche*, the people have great sex, but what you saw was a funeral, so no sex."

I laughed, "It is probably the sex that makes Father Mary think voodoo is so bad. Father Mary also told me that the Governor of Louisiana, one of our states in the United States, prohibited the importation of Negroes from Martinique because of voodoo over two hundred years ago. Voodoo has been a problem for a long time. It is probably the sex."

"So perhaps that was a good idea your governor had, but his reason was wrong. It was not the voodoo that was bad. My people knew voodoo for many years and it was not a bad problem. It was slavery that was wrong. My ancestors were slaves for many years. I am free, but I come from slaves and I think it is wrong for any man to own another man. What do you think, Edward?"

I felt the intensity of the question. It was the same intensity Louis used asking his life or death question.

"You are right, Louis, one man should not own another man. But, it was not the question of slavery that kept these people out, it was voodoo. Father Mary still opposes voodoo and he is a modern man not concerned with the question of slavery. He says, and more than once I heard him say it, he says the natives on Martinique are like children. They are good Roman Catholics on Sunday, but they still practice voodoo the other days of the week."

"So Father Mary is right about our religion, Edward," replied Louis sounding quite stern. "But you will see the healing ceremony for yourself, just as you heard the wise woman for yourself. You must decide if voodoo is bad, harmful or evil and if using it makes us children. Anyway, I have an idea for you to think about while we wait for the healing ceremony to start tonight. Come in to the forest with me and I will show you."

CHAPTER SIXTEEN

"So Edward, I have this enormous good idea," Louis was obviously excited. "You are always asking about our native medicines and I am thinking that I know quite many of them by myself.

"So when you have many children in a family, there were ten in mine, your mother tells you to go and pick a certain berry, or a certain leaf to make your brother or sister well. Is that what you want to know about?"

"So maybe I do not know about the salves that Marie uses, or the teas and broths she makes, no one knows about those things except Marie. However I do know many leaves and berries and such that may be special for you and these I can show you. So I also know that Marie goes out to collect her materials in the afternoon and maybe we can just happen to watch her. Does all of this idea help?"

The excitement was catching. He smiled as I said, "Yes! Yes! That would be a good start. Thank you for thinking of it. I know nothing about natural remedies so show me what you know."

"So I do not know so much, only know what they look like and what they do. I do not know anything more than what any child would know."

"Give me an example." I was eager to explore this idea.

"So a certain leaf boiled in water makes a tea. To get well you drink the tea. Sometimes a leaf goes on a wound by itself. Like if you have a wasp sting, then you get a certain leaf and put it over the sting so the pain is gone and the swelling never comes. There is also a strange shaped white mushroom that grows from a rotting log. You squeeze the juice out of this mushroom and drip it into the ear through a curled leaf. It is for earache. Sometimes this mushroom is very hard to find. You have to go deep into the forest to get it."

"What do you mean by a strange shape, Louis?"

"So a strange shape is not round or perfect at the edges."

"You mean it is irregular?"

"That is it, Edward. Irregular shape. Do you want to hear more?"

"Yes, please."

"A tea for fevers comes from a red berry with a fuzzy green leaf. For centipede stings there is a plant with spokes like a wheel that has berries on the end and in the middle. One used often is a vine with a large flat heart shaped purple flower for stomachaches. There are also plants for coughs and tired eyes. I do not know where some of the more powerful plants come from. Those plants drive off evil spirits— the people who know, like Marie protects those. They also have leaves and bark from a tree with three shiny leaves soaked in cold water to make a drink that lets some very special people talk to the spirits."

"You know quite a lot just by yourself, Louis. I'm impressed. Do these remedies actually work?"

"Usually they work, but I do not know how they compare to your medicines, Edward. Anyhow for us they work good enough."

"Someday, someone will come to study the native ways here because your natural healing is amazing. We have taken many of our medicines from plants, but now we seem to be looking more at the chemistry." I pondered as an idea formed. Maybe the wise woman meant my new work was to learn how they used the plants here. Out loud I said, "How you use medicine that you make from plants is outstanding. There is a great deal that we can learn from you."

"Learn from us? Edward, you must be making a joke with me. So let us go exploring the in forest. Start to practice walking quiet, then when we see Marie we can watch her without her hearing us. We can whisper and talk now though." Louis turned to me, "So, Edward, what will you do?"

"About what?"

"About what the wise woman said."

"You heard her. The wise woman says I will find a wife going home on the ship and become an editor once I am back. I don't think this will happen. Maybe this idea about learning healing plants is what she meant."

"What is an editor?"

"He goes over other peoples' work before the newspaper or magazine prints it."

"Edward, that is interesting, but it is not exactly what I meant when I asked what you will do. I want to know what will you do about bamboche. She said we were not to go to the bamboche."

"I don't know. Everyone else is going if they do have one. That leaves us by ourselves. What will we do, Louis?"

"I will go," growled Louis. "She should not forbid me. I do not understand why I can't go. I can understand why you can't go, but why should they forbid me? I must talk to Marie when we get back. For now let us look at the leaves."

We quietly walked through the forest, with Louis pointing out different leaves and berries to me. I regretted I had not brought paper to take notes on, or a collection bag of some kind, but Louis reassured me that we would be passing the same plants when we left for Fort-de-France and I could get the same information along that road. The real purpose now was to spy on Marie and what she was collecting.

Suddenly Louis put a finger to his lips and looked around. I also looked around cautiously and caught sight of a brilliant red fabric moving through the trees. Louis motioned me to follow him and moved off to the side of the very faint path they were following.

It was Marie coming down the path. I didn't know if the tall underbrush was enough to hide us, but I didn't have much choice. She stopped about five feet from where we hid and started picking some leaves. We held our breath.

I nodded my head toward Marie and motioned at her with my head while I mouthed, "What's that?" Louis shrugged his shoulders and shook his head. "Don't know," he mouthed back.

As Marie moved slowly along the path gathering different parts of plants, Louis made a mental note of them and nodded "yes" to indicate to me that it was a known plant she was picking. He just frowned if he did not know the plant.

We moved cautiously on a parallel path with Marie. We stepped carefully, deliberately and didn't make a sound. Then the brush cover ran out. We watched from a distance, but fortunately we spotted another undergrowth where we could scurry when she was just out of sight.

I held my breath as we watched Marie move away from us. I started to cross to the other plant cover, but she turned back our direction and I ducked back hoping I did not make a noticeable movement. Louis shook his head and looked disgusted. He moved in front of me. It was obvious that he would do the leading. He knew what he was doing.

Marie started going back the other direction away from us again. After a pause, Louis started across the open stretch of forest heading for new protective cover. I hesitated only a second, then gingerly followed Louis.

It did not take long for us to find Marie again but now she was going off the path and into the woods on the other side. "We have lost her. We can't follow her there," I whispered. Louis put his finger to his lips to hush even a whisper and indicated another parallel path we might take. He started to walk, cautiously as ever, and I followed him with equal caution. Maybe the cover of the trees here would shield us from her sight.

There was sound behind me, wood crackling and then birds angrily squawking. I was startled and my footing was thrown off. I tripped over a root that was sticking out from a vine and landed on the ground with a thud. I looked around. There was no other movement, and I heaved a sigh of relief at remaining undiscovered.

Louis came back to help me to my feet and brush me off. I could walk, nothing was broken. I was just shaken up. I nodded that we could go on and we turned to pick out the path again. We looked up to see Marie blocking our path.

"I am furious with you for spying on me. You will come back with me and you will stay put at our little dwelling until the healing ceremony tonight. I see for myself the problem the wise woman saw. You are both not worthy of trust. There will be no bamboche for sure for either of you. Follow me." She turned on her heel and strode off.

"So we were out for a walk and Edward fell when his foot caught on a branch sticking from the ground," Louis pleaded. "We were doing nothing bad."

Marie ignored him. She walked briskly with a stiff spine toward the shack. We followed sheepishly behind.

Now I knew for sure why I was forbidden to attend bamboche. I was not trustworthy. I did not know with certainty before. I thought there might not be an appropriate woman for me because I was an outsider.

The more I thought about it, the more I decided it wasn't fair. I was not a child to be scolded and put off. After all, the night of uninhibited drinking and lovemaking would show I was ready to return to the outside world. It was an experience I looked forward to. I felt they accepted Louis, but maybe I was still a stranger. I was not one of them and could not learn or share their ways. I was a white man in a black man's world. Then again, Louis couldn't come either.

The natives were friendly. They took care of me. Louis answered all my questions as completely as he could. They seemed to hold no secrets from me. Yet, when they didn't want me to know what they were saying they slipped into the native Creole and abandoned the French I could use to communicate. Being with these people was not the frightening experience I expected. They never threatened or bullied me. They treated me well. They had healed me! These natives were gentle people. I was white and did not belong. Still, this did not explain why Louis was forbidden the bamboche. Was it enough that he was also not trustworthy? After all, he was native to the island. He was voodoo. He was a voodoo mystery! I decided Louis should be furious.

Louis did stomp back into the hut close behind Marie. A word or two in Creole from Marie and everyone left us alone with her. Marie gave Louis a cup of something liquid, which he drank without hesitation. Marie approached me with my cup. Most of the beverages she offered to drink were hot or warm. This was cool. Nevertheless, hot or cold, I was unwilling to drink it.

"Is this a drug to put me to sleep?" I asked. I knew of no reason for this. We could stay put without it.

"Please drink this. It will relax you. You will have a good nap. Please." Marie coaxed as though her anger had subsided when she held the cup out to me.

"I don't want to drink it, thank you. I don't want to be calm and relaxed. I won't be a bad boy." I was adamant. Marie was being childish. Louis was falling asleep.

"We will have a healing ceremony for you. You have tried to follow me and so you deserve nothing more than this. The wise old woman said you should not attend *bamboche*. She saw your evil intent and we cannot permit you to go against her words of wisdom. It will not benefit you. Please drink this." She pressed the cup toward me. "Now."

"Why can't Louis go?" I asked.

Louis turned his half closed eyes to look at me. "You do not understand, Edward," he said softly. "The wise woman is very powerful. She saw our plan. Now I do not dare go against her in anything. She has made it clear that we are not to go. If we try to, it will be very bad for us. We may be back to when they found us in the overturned cart, only this time they will not save us. I want to go too, but I also value my life, such as it is. Drink the liquid. It will not harm you and we still have the healing ceremony."

"Something convinced you that you shouldn't go. What was it Louis?"

"You do not understand how powerful the wise woman is. She can destroy us both. I do not like being forbidden, but possession by a spirit would be worse, and I deserve it. We cannot go, Edward. Drink the liquid and rest now."

I sat impassively. "I just wanted to see what plants you wanted. This may be very important. You don't want to tell me but you didn't say I couldn't see what you use."

Marie placed the cup in my hands quite forcefully. "The choice is yours." Her voice was not coaxing now. It was cold and precise. "I will not force you to drink this. If you do not drink it, I will have to place a guard at the door so you are certain not to disobey my wishes."

It was pointless to refuse. Louis hadn't. There was nothing to gain. If I drank the potion, I was at least assured of a good rest. Reluctantly, I drank the beverage.

The last thing I heard as I drifted into sleep was Louis saying we still had the healing ceremony and that would be good.

CHAPTER SEVENTEEN

I woke up from my long, unwelcome sleep to great activity and laughter. Louis was still sleeping. I went out to ask the ladies how they could be so full of energy after partying all night long. They giggled like young girls and switched to the Creole they spoke when they didn't want me to understand. At last one took sympathy on me and my confusion.

"Mr. Edward, we did not party all of last night. The *Bamboche* was not held. The wise woman said you both made good objections and it was best not to have it at all and to move the healing ceremony to tonight."

Louis emerged from the shack with a yawn to join me and the group of women. Only women surrounded us. I noted these were the same women who were my nurses, my saviors, with one new addition. I saw Marie, young and beautiful, and there was another individual, coffee colored and younger than Marie. She was only a slip of femininity. The two older women were ebony and fat. They

231

chattered constantly when they were together, a sound I had grown accustomed to.

I told Louis, probably with a grumpy voice, "They didn't party last night. We were drugged for nothing." I was aggravated. These women knew how to put me to sleep at their whim. I didn't know if what I was to drink was safe or a soporific.

The women quickly told Louis of the change in plans with the healing ceremony for tonight. At least I think that's what they told him. I was angry at myself, not only was I at the mercy of these women, with all the time I spent on the island I never bothered to learn the local patois. French was the civilized language so why bother?

Louis and I were told to go out walking. Obediently, we circled the shack in widening arcs. We didn't talk. I guess we had nothing to say. We just walked. The weather was fair and we were certainly well rested. It was pleasant to walk. The women's high spirits continued all day and into the afternoon meal preparation.

Marie called out to us. The group was going to eat earlier than usual. "We will eat only a little, and very quickly," said Marie. "Then we will go a little early to the healing ceremony so that you may quiet yourselves and make it good."

I looked at Louis. He knew what she meant. He smiled at me and nodded his head up and down.

Marie turned to look at both of us. "We are having the healing ceremony tonight. You are well rested as planned and if all goes well you may be off to Fort-de-France tomorrow morning."

Dutifully we ate as directed, and finished promptly. Then Louis led me to a shady area not far away, up the mountain a little. I really didn't know just where. Logs were placed around in an attempt to outline a circle. In the center was a fire pit.

'Now what?" I asked Louis.

"So we will make our heads quiet and become ready for the ceremony."

"I don't understand. What do you mean?"

"Edward," he said quietly, with a large smile spreading across his face, "I can teach you something now. This makes me feel good. There is something I know for sure that you don't." He laughed quietly to himself. "Besides learning how to quiet your head is there anything you must know? Any questions for me? You have been good telling me everything, so now I can help you."

"Louis, can you tell me anything about this healing ceremony? Is there a payment I need to make? A charge? Do I owe anything? Is there anything I should do?" I asked Louis.

"So Edward you have to understand the whole system. Curers are what we call people who heal and Marie is more than an ordinary healer. So she is above the curers because she is also a priestess. Part of the work is to give healing ceremonies when they will help. Besides she knows we own nothing, so our thanks is enough. Do not concern yourself about the ceremony. It is something Marie wants to do for us.

"So I will tell you more, explain it if I can, as it is happening and as I remember the meaning. I may not know the meaning of everything, but that is not so important. After all do you know all the meaning in a special mass?"

"No," I answered sheepishly.

"Then, I may not know all the meaning in the healing ceremony. So I will be in good company because you don't know everything about your own ceremonials," Louis chided. "Now what I am going to teach you is very easy to hear, but not so easy to do. Come sit against this tree." He motioned to a large shady tree I didn't recognize. I went and sat down next to him.

"So this is very gentle. You sit and do nothing."

"Do nothing? Why do nothing? I can't do nothing. That is wasting time when I should be doing something. After all we are both well now."

"Edward, that is what makes this hard. It is even harder for you because you must always do something. Now you must do nothing. You must just be." Louis put his finger to his lips to silence me. There was nothing more to say. I was to sit and do nothing for I didn't even know how long.

I was comfortable. Maybe I could take a nap but I didn't feel like napping. I watched the birds. I saw little insects on the soft brown dirt by the tree. I listened to the noises the birds made, singing and rustling among the leaves. I realized if I concentrated enough I could even hear the sounds coming from the tiny insect creatures around me. I heard Louis breathing. I concentrated on my own breathing. In and out very deliberately. I watched my chest rise and fall. This was boring.

"Louis, I can't just sit here doing nothing."

Louis opened his eyes and smiled at me. "So of course you can. I believe you need more help. So close your eyes. Follow my words and I will relax your body. When you are all relaxed you can count as far as you can, or you can take a breath in and out, thinking the word in when you take breath in and out when you send breath out.

"So I will start with your feet. Think about your feet and let them rest as you breathe. Now your lower legs. Keep breathing in and out and let your legs rest. Now think of your upper legs." Louis spoke softly and paused between directions. I felt my body slowing down. I felt warm and comfortable.

"Breath in and out. Let the legs rest. Now your stomach, still breathe in and out and rest. Now your chest. Now your hands. Now your arms. Now your back. Now your neck. Now your head."

I began to count in measured unhurried bits of concentration. I don't know how long this went on. Sometimes I lost count and started over from the last number I remembered. Then a steady, strong drumbeat, with a repeated rhythm, rudely called us from our quiet place to the healing ceremony near by. I felt light and calm. I would say serene even. I never knew such peace before.

I counted to myself, 1-2, 1-2-3, 1-2, 1-2-3 as it continued. The drum invited walking with a distinct style. Without doubt I could detect a certain sway in the movement of the women's hips as they moved ahead of us to the logs around the circle. We had a shared rhythm. I felt it myself.

Our clearing now contained people I had never seen before. There were about two dozen Martinican, men and women in equal numbers, and not a white face among them. I didn't expect to see one.

I was dressed in everyday clothes like all of the men. White cotton pants, a white shirt, no shoes, and a large straw hat to complete the look. At least I was not out of place in my apparel. Some of the men had a long scarf hanging around their necks, all bright colors that matched the women's clothes.

The women were also in the usual garb; wearing vividly colored ankle length dresses of bright reds, oranges, blues and purples. A kerchief or turban wrapped their heads, matching or contrasting with the skirts. They seemed to be wearing more white than usual. The swaying colors were beautiful.

A woman directed Louis and myself to sit on a log beside the fire. When was this fire started? I didn't know. This fire was in the center pit of the circle. Now people surrounded the area. A fire hardly seemed necessary. It would be cooler later, but now it was still quite warm. At least I thought it was.

"I am grateful that it is going to be dark soon," remarked Louis.

"It will be cooler out and this fire won't seem so unnecessary?" I asked, trying to get his meaning.

"No, so people will not stare at me and I am also gratefully thankful for the log to sit on. Because of the drink before my rest, I do not have the energy to stand or dance and to sit on the ground is difficult." Louis settled himself carefully on the log. "Am I saying that right?"

"I know what you mean," I reassured him. "Why do you think they are staring at you?"

"Because I am so ugly and many of these people have not seen me before. Because I have hideous scars on my back and because I lived when everyone else died. They must think that I do not have a right to be the only one to live."

"Louis, what you are saying does not make sense. You are wearing a shirt. No one can see your back and you've told me that this is a healing ceremony. Why would Marie put so much effort into saving someone that does not have a right to live?"

Louis shrugged and turned his body to the side a little. The drumbeat changed. It was softer, slower, and more even in tempo. It invited calm. People murmured quietly and rocked slowly, side to side, or back and forth as they sat on the ground. I joined them in the soothing movement as I invited the calm feeling back into my own body.

"So you are right," said Louis turning back to me and whispering. "This ceremony is for healing. Perhaps my decision is made for me and I am to continue to live, and the people here do not hate me for being alive. This is not a ceremony for spirits. Spirits cause disease. Disease is not our problem. So this ceremony is for healing and I do promise I will tell you what I know about the ceremony.

"So this ceremony is different from place to place and leader to leader and curer to curer. What is here will not be on another part of the island. What Marie does is not the same as what a man might do, or another woman even. It is not one set ritual for one certain thing, like we have in church.

"You see, Edward, we believe that man has a body and his soul gives the body life. The body dies, but the soul does not die. The soul never dies. So see, the soul can become divine or it can go into a living person - possession."

The drumbeat changed again and the group began to chant in Creole as Marie entered the circle wearing a long purple gown. She walked near the drums to a crude cross made of branches. She knelt down and drew something in the dirt. I could not tell what it was.

Louis said quietly, "She is saluting the guardian of the cross roads. She is making the sign of the cross, earth and heaven, body and soul."

Marie approached the drums and the rhythm changed again. She poured something out of a jug sitting near the drummer into small bowls and set them in front of the drums.

"The drum is a sacred object to us," whispered Louis. "We salute it at the beginning and end of each ceremony. There will always be two or three drums. They should have a different sound for each of them so they can play their own music. Soon the dancing will begin. The leader will start and the drummers will follow."

"Are those chants a song or a prayer?" I asked quietly.

"That one now is a prayer, but all dances and main ceremonial acts must have songs. So the prayers are asking for patron spirits to come and help us in our healing, and the offerings are for them too. In a way these spirits are like Father Mary's saints, though he would not like to hear me say this."

"Louis, do you recognize most of these people?"

"No, I know few of them. They work on this part of the island, in the cane fields, and I do not know them. So I work on the other side of the island, fishing in the ocean.

"After tonight I will know them. They will be my brothers and sisters. Hideous and helpless as I am, I will be part of this place. Something that Father Mary does not understand is that voodoo makes us one, a part all mixed together. We become joined. I am not just myself, I am all of us. We become one, a single spirit. The drums bring us together. Having our rituals tells us we are, each of us, the community. Do you understand me, Edward?" asked Louis with a worried frown.

"I think so. You become joined all together in one community, one group. You do things for each other and help each other out." Louis nodded his agreement. "Is sex part of this community idea?"

"Not at a healing ceremony. But in other ceremonies, of course," replied Louis. He seemed dumbfounded that I had asked. "Father Mary thinks it is evil. So to us it is love and makes us all one, which we are. So Father Mary does not understand many things about us.

"He calls it sin when a man and woman mate outside of marriage. Here that is usual until the woman is going to have a child. So then the man and woman agree to live together and we think of them as married. Father Mary does not understand getting married in church costs money."

"Many couples do get married in the way that Father Mary expects, don't they?" I asked.

"Yes, people with money. Many times even poor people save enough to marry, but that is often after many children. Father Mary calls these children bastards, but we know who they belong to, so they are not bastards to us."

Marie entered the circle to show that the ceremony was starting. She began to dance. As she danced, she scattered dried maize, peanuts and cassava around the dancing arena. I let myself sway to the music. I saw that Louis also kept time but closed his eyes. I chose not to close my eyes. I wanted to watch and remember as much as I could about this ceremony.

There was no particular formation for the dancers to follow, though they all went counter-clockwise. Some stayed in the center of the circle and others moved around the edge, or back and forth between the center and the edge. There was considerable movement of the hips and shoulders.

The men danced with their slightly bent arms hanging. Some pulled the ends of the cloth around their necks in time to the drums, the way I would dry my back with a towel.

The women raised the hem of their long skirts and moved the fabric in waves in time to the music and their swaying bodies. The rhythms and songs changed, and the dancers altered their movements for the new song. I was mesmerized by the sound and the movement. I felt quite calm yet uniquely alive and excited, like there was electricity in the air.

Louis turned his attention back to the dancing and I followed his lead. As darkness fell, the men lit torches and the women handed out plates of food and glasses of water.

"This is ritual food. So it will include a quartered, roasted rooster, with its crest and feet. We will not get this to eat, so do not let the idea alarm you. Even though this ceremony is for us, we are not important enough for those special parts," said Louis.

"Is this why the woman was washing the chicken? For the ritual food?" I asked.

"Don't you know the difference between a chicken and a rooster?" answered Louis with a laugh. "She was washing a chicken. I said a rooster was used in this food. The chicken is for the ceremony."

I glanced at my plate. It held rice cooked in milk, greengage jam with a maize biscuit, a fried egg, bananas fried in sugar and mangoes. No chicken, no rooster. I ate with relief. Others also ate, but the dancing continued.

After everyone finished eating, the drums took on a different beat. It started slowly and grew increasingly frenzied. Louis whispered that the sacrifice would come soon. As the drums slowed their beat, the dancers moved back to the edge of the circle clearing a space in the center.

Marie appeared with the freshly bathed chicken I saw earlier. She offered it maize and a glass of water. The chicken was calm and not at all eager to escape. The food did not interest it.

"The chicken must eat and drink to become part of the spirit we need for healing," whispered Louis.

Marie continued to offer the chicken food and at last it ate some grain. Marie lit a candle with a taper from the fire. Louis whispered that the candle was for communication with spirits. After the chicken ate and drank some more, Marie marked it with a cross on its back. I thought she used charcoal to make the cross, but I couldn't see everything plainly. Marie picked the chicken up with both hands and approached us.

"Do not be afraid, Edward. She will just have the chicken walk on us," said Louis.

Walk on us? I did not have time to protest or even question what was happening. Marie brought the chicken over to me and held it, guiding it while it walked up one side of my body, across my head and down the other side. I was aware of the chicken walking over me. I felt little pricks of electricity. I watched as she performed the same rite with the chicken walking on Louis' body.

When Marie moved away, I leaned toward Louis and quietly asked a rush of questions. "Is that bird drugged? Has it been given something to make it feel so stimulating when it walked over us? Why is it cooperating with her? It isn't trying to get away. Why isn't it afraid?"

Louis shook his head slowly back and forth. "I do not know. I have never had the chicken walk on me before. Also I have never seen a chicken so quiet, so willing to let someone handle it. Maybe it is part of Marie's magic."

"Why does she have the chicken walk on us?"

"I do not know," answered Louis, "but I have seen it done many times before."

Marie danced with the chicken and shook it by its legs, like a dirty feather duster. The chicken did squawk and flap its wings at this rough handling, but it did not try to peck at Marie or her imprisoning hands. She lifted the chicken into the air four times. The bird also protested this with loud squawks but did not fight.

"So the four times she shakes the chicken is for earth, heaven, body and soul. Just as the cross represents these things to us," whispered Louis.

I watched this fascinating ritual trying to focus on details of movement. Before I realized what happened, Marie twisted the head off the bird, killing it before it could make a sound. She plucked a few breast feathers out. Using the chicken's blood, she stuck them on the cross of branches. She placed the chicken and its head in front of the drummers. I saw Marie put the bird down, then I didn't see her anymore. Marie disappeared before my eyes.

The drums picked up the strong fast beat again. Marie had disappeared completely. The dancers sang and danced, my body swayed with the drum beats, but the drum songs, after reaching a frenzy, grew slower and slower. The drums faded away at last. The ceremony was over, leaving everyone composed, placid and I suppose tired from the dancing. I felt empty, not tired. I wanted to hear more of the drums. Maybe I should have danced. No one told me I couldn't.

With quiet calm restored all around, Louis and I walked back silently to the shack to sleep. We needed sleep to be stronger in the morning. Strong enough to walk to Fort-de-France if we couldn't get a ride.

Would we be stronger tomorrow? Did this ceremony mean something to our welfare as everyone said? Louis knew the ceremony would help us, but I didn't know, or believe, any ceremony could help. Yet I sensed something within me had changed.

We both knew we needed more sleep and sleep would help us even if the ceremony didn't. We did not know what tomorrow would bring, but we looked forward to finding out. We gratefully accepted the warm bowls of broth the women offered. Sleep was gentle and quieted our minds, much as Louis had calmed me before the ceremony. Tomorrow would be good.

CHAPTER EIGHTEEN

I was the first to wake up. I stretched my legs out then my arms. A tremendous yawn felt good. I glanced around the room. Everyone was sleeping soundly as if they had been the ones drugged last night. I slipped quietly from my bed to go outside without disturbing the stillness.

It was another perfect day. We should have more rain, but maybe the erupting volcano changed the usual weather pattern. In any case, it was perfect outside and I felt fit enough, and aware enough, to enjoy it. I was ready to travel back to civilization and today was the day.

I decided to wait on the porch for the others to wake up and join me. These people were early risers, weren't they? I didn't know. Maybe my thinking was wrong and they weren't early risers. Maybe it was an extraordinary ceremony and it would take a lot of extra sleep to make up for the festivities. When it came down to it, I didn't know much about these people at all. It didn't make any difference now. Today I was going back to civilization.

I had lost more than a month of my time, but I was alive after my harrowing accident and I had a prophecy to go with my restored life. My experience with these Negro people was unique. It was not what I expected.

They didn't ignore me, or mistreat me. They fed me and acted like I might be one of them, with the exception of denying me *bamboche*. Without a doubt, they had healed me. I had survived a brutal accident because they cared for me, even though I was not one of them. Just seeing how Louis Ciparis' burns had healed was an extraordinary revelation.

I should still pursue the exact method, how it was done, what it was done with, somehow, someway, someday. Or at least I should persist enough to discover the ingredients that Marie used to heal those burns. Even if it meant one extended trip, or many trips back to the island at some point. Louis said it was hopeless, but he would try to learn what he could from the other women. What valuable information that could be. There would be a good story there when I sorted everything out. Maybe not the story I expected, but good information nonetheless. Maybe a lost month or two was not a bad exchange for what I gained.

The early morning sunshine was welcome, but I wanted a good cup of coffee, fresh ground from the native beans. Louis appeared. He shuffled by me with a nod of acknowledgment.

It occurred to me that in some ways Louis looked only slightly better today than the first time I saw him. It was true that he was not bleeding from deep burns, or oozing ugly pus, but his head bowed with weight of a different sort now. The healing ceremony was successful so now he had to go back and begin living his life again.

There was noise in the cottage as people came to life. I could smell fresh coffee brewing and waited with anticipation. Louis came to the shack to sit beside me.

"So they will bring us coffee and a special bread for energy." Louis dropped his head to rest on his arms. His effort at speech was a tiring one this morning.

"So why am I so very tired after a successful healing ceremony?" He looked at me sadly. I don't think he was expecting an answer.

"What's in the bread?" I questioned. I was eager to learn something new.

"I do not know," muttered Louis, barely raising his head. "I do not care," he mumbled on. "I only know it helps make you feel more alive."

Marie appeared with a tray filled with steaming coffee mugs and slices of bread. The ceremony did not tire her. She looked as calm and beautiful as usual. Perhaps even a little more vibrant. Louis took his mug and slice of bread appreciatively.

"I was waiting for this. This is the bread I just told you about, Edward." Louis began eating the bread with great expectations about its energy giving qualities.

"You take some also," Marie offered me the tray. "It will not hurt you. It will give you energy for your long trip."

"What's in it that will give me energy?"

"It is a very good food, carefully made. It gives energy. It helps heal. Try some."

"Does it have special ingredients?"

"Of course it does. It is my special bread."

"It's a good thing to have energy from bread. Could I learn how to make it?"

Marie laughed. "No. It is my special bread. I <u>never</u> reveal my secrets to anyone. <u>Never</u>." Marie said this in such a way that her answer cut off the idea of any further questions.

The secret ingredients for the bread, the secret ingredients that healed Ciparis and the secret ingredients in his new cream, were just that. Secret. What a pity she wouldn't tell. Many people would benefit, but she would lose her power. Louis told me Marie would not give up her power. At least I tried again.

"So, do Louis and I go to Fort-de-France today?" I inquired, already knowing the answer.

"Yes, after you eat the morning meal. It is unfortunate, but you will have to walk. The owner of the plantation and his family have gone to Fort-de-France. Only the servants remain. The workers who haul the produce to market have not returned yet."

"How far is Fort-de-France from here?"

"It takes about two hours of brisk walking for a healthy man. No more than that. For you, if you do not walk briskly, it will take longer, maybe four hours. That gives you an idea of how long it will take. When you connect with the main road, you will probably get a ride," assured Marie cheerfully.

I looked at the sun streaming through the palm trees. "It is a perfect day for a walk," I said. "Then again, I thought it was a stunning day for a ride when we left Morne Rouge and look where that ride got me - in an accident and a month missing from my life."

"So this time we will have a large knife to protect us," offered Louis. "You will have the kind used to cut the cane after the workers burn it off and Marie is going to give each of us a strong charm for protection."

"That's right," said Marie. "I will go now to get your charms and other things for you to take with you."

I said pointedly, "Louis, you had strong charms before and they didn't do much good."

"But those charms were not from Marie. So I think she is most powerful. My people are taking very excellent good care of you and me. Now we even get a special charm. I believe I know this charm. It is a very particular, very strong charm. This honors both of us. This charm will protect us for much longer than the walk to Fort-de-France. Maybe I should ask her for something to help my manhood." Louis glanced at his feet. "No. It is better for me to ask in the city from someone I do not know."

Reluctantly I asked, "Why do you think you have a problem?"

"I see these beautiful women and I do not feel anything. I thought I might and that is why I wanted so much to *bamboche*, but making love and drinking and having fun are so far away from me now. I do not feel like a man. Before, I would have thought about what a woman might feel like. Was her skin as soft as it looked or does it look soft but is really rough? I would want to know how her mouth would taste. Now, I do not care. It would shame me to have her feel my skin. To feel my body. I wonder if I will ever be a man again."

"Look, Louis, wouldn't it hurt to have anyone touch your skin right now anyway? Isn't your skin still a little tender and easily scratched and broken? Isn't your skin fragile because it's so new? It is like a baby's skin only even more sensitive.

"Give yourself some time. It's incredible that these herbs, or whatever Marie used, healed you so fast. You should, by rights, still have blisters covering your burns. When I saw you two weeks after the eruption, you were not healed at all. You were oozing blood from your wounds. At least give yourself the usual time it would take to heal, many months, before you worry about what you can and can't do. Have you forgotten what the wise woman told you?"

"So you are right, Edward" said Louis glumly. "I am impatient and I am to learn to be patient." He got up and took his cup inside.

A woman came out to take my cup. She gave me a bag with pineapple, bananas and bread for the walk. Marie came out with Louis and placed a small bag, with a twine tie, over his head, like a necklace. Then she put one over my head. I recognized the distinctive odor of basil. It smelled fresh, with a stimulating earthy odor.

"Edward, I have given some thought to what you said about wanting my secrets so that many people can benefit. I have an idea." Marie paused, keeping me on edge. "If you learn enough about natural healing plants, enough to talk to me wisely, then come back and I will talk with you. But now is the time to say good-bye." She left before either of us had time to respond.

"Louis, is she joking?" I didn't accept her change of heart. She must be joking.

"So I don't know. I've never heard such a thing before. It is most strange."

While we were giving this new response considerable thought, a man came out from the trees to lead us to the road. There were no farewells. Everyone disappeared. He left us without a sound when we reached the road. Louis and I started walking to Fort-de-France on a one-lane road lined with tree ferns and bamboo. Our unhurried pace was steady. For a while there was silence between us.

Finally I broke the silence. "I feel as if I didn't say farewell properly. These people probably saved my life. I didn't get a chance to thank them. I'll probably never see them again, even if I try. I only know Marie's name. I don't know who they are or where they are from. I feel I've left something undone."

"No, Edward. It is enough for them to see you walking away a healthy man, just as it is enough for me to leave. That tells them something. It tells them they have succeeded. So they know we respect what they have done for us. Here in the island, things are done and no one needs thanks. Someday you will be able to help someone else and you repay what they have done for us by doing something for that person. That person repays what you do by helping someone else. This goes on and on. This circle of help is the thanks my people want."

A noise in the undergrowth startled Louis. He nervously grabbed at the knife I was carrying. A bird flew up into a tree and Louis laughed with relief.

"I should not be so jumpy. It is not like me." Louis hesitated. "Maybe it is like me now, but it is not like I used to be. I want to stop and use some of the cream that Marie gave me." We stopped in the shade at the side of the road. Louis removed his light white cotton shirt and applied the salve.

"So I think they have sent us off to be rid of us. I think they will have *bamboche* tonight. We do not have to go just because they sent us. We can stop here and later in the afternoon circle back. What do you think?"

"I think it is probably not a good idea."

Louis looked a little downcast. "You are right, but I hoped maybe it should be different. Anyway, I can show you plants as we go. You can start learning so you can come back some day and see if Marie jokes with you."

Louis got to his feet. "Let us go now." We set off at a brisk pace as Louis continued to talk. "Marie told me that I will always be sensitive to heat and cold now. I cannot get too hot or too cold. So I do not know why she told me about cold. It does not get so cold here that I should worry. It gets cool, but not cold."

"Don't you remember what the wise old woman said?" I countered. "She said you would go away on a ship. Maybe you will go to a cold place, or at least a colder place."

"Maybe that is the reason Marie warned me," said Louis.

"Forget warnings. This is a beautiful road, isn't it? Will our walk be through a forest like this all the way to Fort-de-France, or do we go as far south as the bare rocks and white sand?"

"No, Edward, we do not go that far south at all. They would not let me leave if I would get too much sun. It will be much like this forest most of the way to Fort-de-France."

"This isn't really a forest to me. It's more like a jungle. At home, near Boston, our forests smell fresh, clean. This smells heavy and dark. It smells of life and death, of sweetness and decay. It's a jungle."

"So I would rather be outside and smell this than in a small dark room smelling ash and burning flesh. I am sorry, Edward, I fear I will need many stops to rest. I am not as strong as I thought I was. Maybe it is my mind that is not strong because I do not want to be back with people. I should be happy I can walk by myself. It is many weeks ago and yet I still wonder why I am alive at all. Do you know, Edward? Why am I alive?"

"I don't know. Even the wise woman said she didn't know. You were in the path of a catastrophe, but something protected you somehow. It is not as though the eruption didn't touch you. You were severely burned. Your burns are the price you paid. For you, the price was not your life."

"I need to rest again."

We sat down again in the shade at the side of the road. For starting at such a good pace, the stops came close together now.

"Do you want something to eat or drink?" I shoved the bag of provisions toward Louis.

"No. So I still just need to rest and talk about what happened to me again. You know, I always expected to be with my mother when she died but I was not with her. No one was with her and yet everyone was with her. I feel I do not have a part of her, or anyone, with me now. I was not truly there in the city. I was not part of what happened. You are a good person to talk to, Edward. Do you know that?"

"I get paid to listen to people. That's part of my job. I'm glad you think I'm a good person to talk to, but why do you think so?"

"You are a stranger. You do not know what I was like, so you do not judge me. I can tell you many things, because I will not live with you near me and you cannot tell anyone who knows me. I can show you that I am struggling and I do not know what to think. I can tell you I wonder if I will ever dream beautiful dreams again. There is something else. You do not have to save me, or my soul. Father Mary might listen to me, but he has a need to save my soul. You do not have any interest in me."

"But I do. The wise woman saw it. She said I should not be jealous of the new chance at life that you have. She said we all have a chance to change our lives. I do have an interest in you. I want to see what you do with this second chance at life. I want to hear what you decide about all this. I want to learn from you. You are a survivor."

Louis laughed. "You have education. You can read and write. So what can you learn from me?"

I smiled back at Louis. "I'm not sure."

"You say I am a survivor, yet don't forget when everyone else returns to their lives mine will still lie in shreds, like a broken plate with missing pieces. The plate can never fit together again because some of the pieces are gone forever. I feel more like a victim than a survivor."

"I guess in a way you are a victim," I agreed reluctantly. "You've had an overwhelming loss from a force that you had no control over. That makes you a victim. But you are alive when others died, and that makes you a survivor. You are both, a survivor and a victim. Making you a survivor, instead of a victim, is more positive."

Louis laughed at this. "Yes, let us try to be positive and let us try to walk some more. We should go slower. So I may need one more stop before we get close enough to catch a ride going in."

"Do you think we can get a ride?"

"So I'm sure of it."

"Do I need to carry this huge clumsy knife until then?"

"I would feel better if you did," said Louis. "There might not be any people around to help us if a fer-de-lance should appear." Again Louis laughed. The idea wasn't funny at all to me. I decided that carrying the heavy knife was not so objectionable. I did not know what was ahead of us. Maybe another snake. Maybe not. Why not be prepared.

CHAPTER NINETEEN

We began our casual walk through the forest in the light and shadows cast by the sun. Again I felt the landscape all around enfolding me. I had a comfortable feeling. If Louis found any good plants, I would collect them. Now that we had decided to go on, and not back, there was more than one purpose. We would get to Fort-de-France and I would have the start of my plant collection. Maybe this was what I should be doing anyway. Why not start now. I could always press dry plants, but it would be a big trip to come collect them fresh. With this decided we could walk and talk.

"Tell me again, Louis, how can you be voodoo and Catholic? Father Mary finds the practice of voodoo quite distressing."

"So we do not make a division between things of the earth and things of the spirit like Father Mary does. We do not call it voodoo. Voodoo is the white man's word. To us one either serves the spirits or does not serve the spirits. For you I will call it voodoo," laughed Louis.

"So anyway, if I must try to separate them for you, I would say voodoo is for my body and being Catholic is for my soul. You can tell from your own experience, and from looking at my burns, that voodoo is for healing. It is for a better life. It makes a strong group of people when we are together. It binds us.

"So Father Mary tells me being Catholic is for my soul," continued Louis. "An angel don't need a charm, but a man does. Voodoo is from the family of the spirits. All the saints are part of voodoo. It is very hard for me to separate these things. Father Mary sees the spiritual only. He sees it apart from the earth. What we do in a worldly way he thinks of as evil.

"Our dancing is a ceremony to invite the spirits to enter our bodies. We truly bring the spirits into our body, yet he says this is heathen. It is not enough of the spirit for him. It is not heavenly. To me there is nothing more of the spirit than inviting them into my body. There is nothing more heavenly. He does not understand our ways. Do you know there was voodoo going on that you did not know, even though you were in the room?"

"No, there wasn't," I replied with heavy doubt in my voice. "I didn't see any voodoo. I didn't see anything strange. I saw your unusually rapid healing, maybe my own healing. The visit with the wise woman, was that voodoo?"

"No. I mean in the room while Marie was healing you," prompted Louis.

"I didn't see any voodoo that I am aware of."

"You did not see some of the things that are important to voodoo because you did not know where to look," said Louis. "The women had a fast for you. Under Marie's instruction, they said special prayers for both of us. After I got better, they sent me out of the hut while they were doing the prayers."

"I wasn't aware of that at all," I admitted. "Since I am up and walking to Fort-de-France, I guess it worked. The wise woman said you needed to bring order and control back into your life. Will voodoo help you do this? Will it bring order and control back?"

"I thought it might, Edward. Then my own people would not let me bamboche and the wise woman did not give me the answer. There is an answer you know. There is an explaining. She would not tell me.

Now I don't know." Louis sighed. "I think I will never get over my loss. I think I must cry when I want to because sometimes I will not want to be strong. I need to learn to live with my loss and know I have lost everything. Do you think I need some order, some routine to my life?" Louis asked me after a pause.

"Yes, Louis, of course. We all need routine. It might be especially good for you. Because it is routine, you do whatever needs doing, but you can think what comes next while you do it. You can think of other work, other ideas. It is very important for you. Especially right now. She is right. It will give you control over your life again. It will show that you can deal with anything."

"So it may be good for me, only I don't know what my routine is any more."

"When you discover it again, it will probably show you what a good life is. What was your routine before, Louis?"

"I would get up and eat and see what kind of day it was. Then I would go down to the quay and see if anyone needed help either fishing or loading or unloading ships. I would work, then go home and eat. Or I would meet some friends and go to eat and drink and party."

"Can you do this in Fort-de-France?" I asked.

"Yes, but first I need to be much stronger. Father Mary told me to go to the big cathedral and get help there until I could take care of myself. He did not know I would be healed. He thought I would still need help. I think that is what I still will do. So I don't know what else to do anyway. Will you go back to your home?"

"Yes, Louis, as soon as possible and remember the wise woman said I would find my wife on the boat. Since you believe what the wise woman says, you agree this is going to happen. I'm looking forward to this eventful meeting with my future wife."

"So do not make fun. When it happens you will feel foolish for not believing. I do not know what I am looking forward to. Right now I feel nervous and anxious. I do not want to be in a small room ever again. I do not want ash near me. It will be a long time before I can go to St. Pierre. I feel so hollow. I am so sad. I have no joy now. It has all been taken from me. Do you understand, Edward?"

"I can understand why you don't want to go to St. Pierre. When you do go there, it will remind you of your injuries and loss all over again. That trip is something you should put off until you are very strong."

"You know we call her the wise woman, but she is more than that. She is a seer. She knows the past and the present, and the future. She is very powerful."

"And you believe her, right?"

"Yes, Edward. She is always good. I have heard about her work for many years. She has always been honest. She has never been wrong. It was an honor to have her talk to me. It was an honor for you also, though you do not know it yet. She is important. She sees me going away on a boat. I guess I should get well and find out about this boat. I wonder where it will go?"

"Well, Louis, perhaps this boat will bring you to the United States and Boston and we can visit. I'll give you my address in case this should ever happen."

"I cannot read or write, but I can have someone else write to you for me."

"Please do that, Louis. Especially when you find the meaning of life," I teased.

Louis laughed. "It will be funny if I find out and you don't. You are the one that can read and write. Right now, right this minute, what do you think the meaning of life is?"

"It will take considerable thought for me to give you any answer to that noble question."

"Then you can think while riding," said Louis gleefully pointing to a cart coming toward us.

I reluctantly put the plant samples collected in my notebook into a pack. There would be no more information or specimens this day. I felt sad about this, but a ride had materialized and we are not doing well walking. I guess we are not as healthy as we thought.

Louis signaled the lumbering wagon to stop as it approached us along the main road our side branch joined. The signal surprised the black driver, who eyed us curiously. I didn't know if that was because the driver was not expecting to see anyone at all let alone a black man and a white one. The perplexed driver invited me to hop onto the back, while he asked Louis to climb in next to him.

"No, thank you," answered Louis to the proffered front seat. "I wish to be near my friend. Can you drop us off at the cathedral?"

The man nodded yes. Louis came to the back of the cart and sat next to me and the cart went bumping off toward Fort-de-France.

"What will you do in Fort-de-France, Louis?"

"I will get myself as completely well as possible and then try to find out if any of my relatives are still living. It would be remarkable if any of them are. I believe they are all dead, but I should be certain. I want to see if they had proper burials, if it was possible."

"Louis, I have another question. The sex at bamboche, what is it like? Did I miss something special? Should we have gone back?"

"Sex is sex. It is wonderful. Father Mary thinks it is evil that we love each other this way. He does not understand this ties us together. So it makes us very close. It is a sharing that makes us all one. Not going back is probably good. When you come again to the island, maybe then."

The rocking motion of the cart put us both to sleep until the cart came to an abrupt stop in front of the cathedral. The jolt woke us up.

"I am home," said Louis with a shrug.

"Let me go in with you and get some paper from the priest so I can give you my address."

"Yes, that is a good idea but you haven't answered my question, Edward."

"What question?"

"What do you think is the meaning of life right this minute?"

"I am not sure what life means, what the purpose is. What a question!" I wanted to go inside, but Louis found a bench and sat down. I joined him.

"What do we need in life?" Louis asked. "Take your time to answer me."

I settled more comfortably on the bench and gave his question some thought. "Louis, it seems to me that all men need recognition and acceptance by the people around them and we need work to do. These are essentials that tell us we are alive. Given this, I think that people do the best they can to get through life comfortably. Is that an answer to your profound question?"

"Yes, it is an answer, but is it the right one? I need to find out. It is important to me."

"Louis, I believe that one day we shall meet again and we may have some answers by then. In the meantime, you have a good question for the priests."

"So you will come back to the island and find me? And some more plants?"

"Perhaps. But, remember the wise woman said you would travel. Maybe you will come to me in Boston."

We stood up and walked into the cathedral. Louis was warmly welcomed. We embraced.

"Good-bye and God bless us both," were Louis' parting words to me.

I headed to the city center to find a way home and if I believed the wise woman I'd also find a wife.

CHAPTER TWENTY

Even in the clutter of mail on my desk, the colorful orange and red scroll design on the edges of the envelope caught my eye. The handwriting was plain, childlike, but firm and bold. My curiosity aroused, I slit open this envelope first. The unusual letter was in simple English.

"Dear Edward, I proud I learn to write in English. I practice as circus gets ready for travel. I come to Boston June 8-13. I want to see you. Louis Auguste Ciparis."

Both the note and the colorful stationery told me Louis Ciparis had joined the circus. A smile flitted across my face as I tucked the bright paper back in the vivid envelope. The postmark was April 1, 1903, New York.

I remembered the wise woman we spent an afternoon with. She said Louis would leave the island and take a risk to have his wishes fulfilled. Obviously Louis had left the island to join the circus to earn money for the boat he wanted. I knew it was not curiosity Louis had about the rest of the world away from the island. I also took the seer's

275

advice, which Louis had no way of knowing. We would have a great quantity of information and changes to discuss when we met again.

I turned enthusiastically to my calendar. Maybe I could go to New York now. There was such a lot to talk about! I would tell Louis how I met my wife on the ship coming back to the United States, as the seer had predicted. I knew my wife before her first marriage. When we met again, on the ship, she was a young, blonde widow.

I took the wise woman's advice completely to heart because I married and became a part-time editor. I was now sitting behind a desk and not out collecting material and writing articles. I changed my career without anyone ever detecting I was a fraud, pretending to feelings and understanding I never had. I was making an effort to overcome my aloofness and coldness as well.

Moreover my wife and I collected plants. We were learning to identify them and their possible healing values. I had not told my wife much about my experience, but I did tell her about how Louis' burns healed. She was willing to learn with me and willing to go to Martinique one day. No details about Marie or Louis ever came out in conversation. Was I avoiding it?

I was genuinely happy to get to see this fellow again. One quick look at my calendar and the circus schedule Louis enclosed, and I knew I had to be patient. The meeting would have to be in Boston in June. I wanted very much to know what was happening to my friend and to share what had happened to me since we parted in Fort-de-France.

I couldn't take my wife to our meeting. She did not know the details of my time with Ciparis, except to say natives cared for me after an accident. She knew nothing of the voodoo, the wise woman or the extent of my injuries or of Louis'.

She would not believe the story anyway. It was unnatural. She was traditional in her thinking. She would not think of anything so out of the ordinary as being normal or natural, only unnatural or abnormal. It would surprise and probably shock her to realize I valued Louis, a Negro man, as a friend not just an acquaintance. She would not understand that I had been a white man in a black man's world and now my friend was a black man in a white man's world.

Maybe I was underestimating my wife. There was a certain adventurous spirit about her. She was learning about plants, collecting them, identifying the leaves and knowing what they might be good for quite willingly. She never complained and frequently had good ideas about how to test the plants for their effects.

My thoughts turned from this reaction concerning my wife to focus on Louis. What could Louis be doing? He must be part of the museum exhibit. Most likely in a replica of his cell, with his scarred back exposed. Louis certainly didn't have any circus talents, like acrobatics or horseback riding. He didn't have any skills that I knew of. Louis had worked as a farmer's helper or a fisherman, very basic work. He was a very simple man.

All Louis wanted was a boat. He wasn't sure how to get that because he didn't have any education or particular talents. And he was physically weak. He was no longer the man he was before the eruption. He must have regained his strength by now. And, being with the circus would give Louis the money for his boat. That was the only reason for him to join the circus. I just knew it. Work in the circus, then buy a boat with what he earned.

There was one other question I would have to answer before our meeting. Where could I take Louis for private conversation and a drink? Certainly a reporter on the city desk would know where a white man and a black man could be comfortable together.

When the day for the visit came, I managed to get away from my desk in the early afternoon. The circus parade through the city was in the morning, so if Louis had been with that parade, he would be back by now. It didn't make sense to put him in the parade. Walking with his shirt on made no sense. Louis would not be in the parade because people would pay to look at his back. With his face unscarred, people wouldn't believe he could be worth the price to look at, unless they were curious about his story.

As I arrived at the circus grounds, workers were adding the finishing touches for the first performance that evening. The bright afternoon light exposed that there was nothing romantic or colorful about the circus. These garish yellows and greens existed nowhere else but here. The paint was still passably fresh, but the strident bright colors were beyond belief. Someone gave some thought to having afternoon performances only in the big top. In a tent, with oil lamps and dim lights, the circus was more enjoyable than it would be if exposed to the honest light of day.

The placard showed Louis Ciparis (Ludgar Sylbaris according to the poster) standing with his hands at his side, holding his white hat with his left hand. He was wearing long white pants, a long-sleeved white shirt and no shoes. This picture was quite authentic in depicting the native dress. The poster proclaimed, "See the only living object in the silent city where 40,000 died."

I bit my lower lip in anger. Louis was not an object. He was a man. It was not 40,000 but 30,000 and that was just the best guess. No one would ever know exactly how many had perished. At least they were not emphasizing the scars from the burns. They were emphasizing the survival.

Inside the tent, as I guessed, there was a replica showing the inside of the cell Louis had survived in. It had three walls, one with a high grated widow, and a heavy wood door braced with steel bands. I found Louis stretched out taking a nap on the rough wood bed inside the cell.

"Hello, old friend," I whispered. I did not want to startle Louis, but I did. His eyes flew open. He started to sit up and in the dim light he made a move to protect himself should his visitor prove unfriendly.

"Edward, is that you?" Louis jumped to his feet and embraced me. "You gave me a fright. Come. Sit." Louis motioned at the wooden bed. He sat down and I joined him.

"I saw the poster. Your name is different."

"Yes, on the poster it is different. My last name is the same name only spelled differently. The first name, I don't know why they changed that. I guess the circus people thought their spelling was more important, maybe better or something."

"Is this new name a problem for you?"

"No, it isn't. The circus people I work with call me Louis, so I feel at home. It is outsiders who want to speak to me in French are a problem, but most call me monsieur and my last name. They are very polite. They always ask the same questions. So I explain again and again how the dungeon protected me. That I was in jail for a minor crime. It is hard work. To repeat yourself again and again is difficult."

"I'll bet they ask you for more specific information about the crime. Circus goers will not let you off just saying a minor crime. You probably have to explain the crime to them don't you?

"Sometimes they do ask me and they do have to ask me otherwise I say nothing. So when they ask me for more information I say that I came in late from a work detail and they wanted to punish me and make an example of me, so they put me in a cell for very important criminals." Louis laughed at the thought. "That usually satisfies everyone. They don't ask what got me in jail in the first place. They have heard rumors and that is enough for them. Probably the same rumors you heard, that I am a murderer, and so they are afraid to ask me. Did you write about me? What did people say?"

"I did write about you, several times. The response was very good, but I didn't win a prize or any fame for my effort. I thought there would be a reaction to the information about the natural plants, whatever Marie used to heal you. But, the physicians here didn't believe me. I did get great satisfaction from writing the articles though. It's that satisfaction that made the effort worthwhile. How do you like circus life, besides answering the same questions?"

"So before I answer your question, Edward, let me tell you about Father Mary. Have you heard about him?"

"Not since I left the island."

"Mont Pelee looked like it was going to erupt again. So officials told everyone to leave Morne Rouge. The scientists studying the volcano felt Morne Rouge might be terribly buried this time. Worse than the usual dust that covered it from other eruptions. So on the evening of August 30, Mont Pelee did erupt again. The eruption sent a lava flow to Morne Rouge and it killed everyone. No one left, including Father Mary, not one person. So it destroyed the people, the little village itself, everything was destroyed as totally as it destroyed St. Pierre.

"Father Mary died in the hospital in Fort-de-France from the burns he got during the eruption. It is hard to believe that burns killed him. I survived with burns that were worse than his. His burns were not so very bad, yet he died in pain. He had been so kind to me with my injuries, I thought maybe there was some way to help him. I was with him when he died. At the end, he didn't even know me. The nurses thought I was just one of his parishioners and didn't let me that close to him. It was very sad."

"I am sorry to hear this, Louis. I did know about the eruption, but not about Father Mary. I assumed he left the area. Did others outside Morne Rouge die as well?"

"Yes, the whole area, some 1,500 to 2,000 people altogether. I didn't know there were that many in Morne Rouge. So I thought most had abandoned the village long ago. Maybe some felt safe, since some time had gone by, and they went back. Why they didn't leave when they were warned I do not know. I saw only a few people when I left Morne Rouge to go to Fort-de-France with you. Did you notice many people?" asked Louis.

"The only people I saw were servants to Father Mary and those who came with you to the wagon after the voodoo ceremony. I didn't see that many people at all in the whole time I was there. Had they come back to the village when the volcano became quieter?"

"So I don't know," replied Louis. "That is the only possibility that makes sense to me. I did not see so many people and you did not see so many people, so they must have come back after we left."

"Poor Father Mary. He stayed until the end. You know that is what he wanted," I replied. "He told me the people who couldn't leave needed him to care for them and that is why he stayed."

"He was a good man," said Louis. "He helped many. Many ill people, or old people who couldn't do much anymore. So he tried to help me. He gave me a little paper with a saying on it. I had a priest read it for me. So that is what got me interested in reading and writing."

"Father Mary was a good man," I agreed. "He died just the way he wanted to, doing his work with the people he cared for. In any case, I was happy to get your letter. Who taught you to read and write?"

"People in the circus help me now, and before, the priests in Fort-de-France. So do you want to hear the saying Father Mary gave me?"

"Of course I do, Louis."

"It is a saying of Saint Francis de Sales. It goes, *'Be patient with every one. But above all with yourself. I mean, do not be disturbed because of your imperfections, and always rise up bravely from a fall.'* I like that. Do you like it?"

"I like it very much, Louis. Father Mary was a good man. Many will miss him. Have you ever gone back to St. Pierre?"

"No. I have never had a reason to go back there. I suppose that someday I will, but so far it has not been necessary."

I smiled. I would probably not go back myself under the circumstances. "Now tell me about circus life, Louis."

"So it is good in some ways and bad in some ways," answered Louis. "I will get the money that I want for my boat when I go back to Martinique, or to another island."

"So you do get your boat! I thought so. I remember the wise woman telling you to leave the island, take a chance and get what you want. You did it. Congratulations." I slapped Louis lightly on the shoulder then was startled at my insensitivity. Was Louis still tender? Had I hurt him?

Louis saw the look of distress on my face. "No, you did not hurt me. I am quite completely healed. I do not like the sun much, but my scars actually make my skin quite strong."

"I am glad to hear that. You know, I tried at great length to get doctors here interested in trying to find the natural plants that healed you so well, or to learn some of the methods that helped me. They just don't believe me.

"Maybe I'll bring them here and let them see you. That probably won't convince them either. They didn't see you just after your ordeal and there are no pictures I know of. I don't want to give up on the idea of the natural medicine, but I'm not getting very far. Perhaps it is an idea I should just forget. Maybe someday, someone will look to the jungle for healing. I am working on learning about plants. I will take Marie up on her offer when I know she is willing to teach me. So, tell me more about the circus, Louis."

"Edward, it is strange. People pay money to see me. So in this make believe cell, I am barefoot. I wear short pants and no shirt so they can see the scars. I can understand why they would pay to see the people on the trapeze, or on the horses, but why would they want to look at me? They call me a human oddity. People will pay to see me because of all the scars on my body. That is what marks me as a survivor.

"At home they can see me for free. They don't find it such an exciting experience to see an unusual person. I don't find it so special.

So I wouldn't pay to see myself. If I knew people would pay for it, I could make up my own circus just for Martinique - from its own people. We have human oddities all around. They are people trying to live as best they can. You Americans are strange. To see a beautiful naked woman is worth money. These places in New York where women dance and remove their clothes so gracefully, that is worth money. That is beautiful. What do you think? Would you pay money to see something ugly when you can see something beautiful?"

I had to agree. "You are probably right. It does make more sense to see the beautiful women than to see strange ones. Does it bother you to be so exposed to strangers?"

"No. So the people, they should be ashamed to pay money to see me," laughed Louis.

"How do you like traveling with the circus?"

"Sometimes we stay a long time in one place. In New York City, where we started, we stayed over a month. I like that. So there is some time to learn about the place. Your places here are so different. So I would not have imagined in my most wildest thoughts how the world is away from my home. Even if I went to school forever, I would not understand. The weather is so strange. So they say it is summer here in Boston. They know because there is no snow, like they have in winter. I tell the difference on the island because we have rain and maybe storms. So we never have snow and it is always warm, but not so hot as it is here. I can use one bunch of clothes in Martinique. Here that is not so. And I need shoes. I don't like shoes. So I will be happy when I can take them off all the time forever. I don't know how you wear shoes, but I see why you need them.

"So anyway, sometimes we stay in one place, other times each day is a different place. This is very hard work. They expect me to help set up the tents and get things ready. That is, tents beside my own tent that I work in, like the big tent. So we all work together to help. No single man can do it alone. So I like that. I like working with a group of people to get something done.

"I get three meals each day, a place to sleep and store my belongings, money and help if I get sick or have an accident. There is always someone who can help me. So the food is tolerably good, but it is unusual for me. It is not what I am used to.

So they have some rules, but they are ordinary and not hard to follow. Some of them are harder than others. You cannot gamble or drink in the tents or the sleeping cars or anywhere around the circus. Remember the hours I work? The hours I am on display and available to talk to people? They are long hours."

I nodded my head. I understood Louis was talking about at least ten hours on a performance day, probably more.

Louis continued, "So wouldn't a good rum drink be pleasant before I go to bed? Or before I go on display? I can't have it. During the day when we are set up, there is nothing to do and we can't gamble. Some games are fun, but it is more exciting if there is a little money involved. Not a lot of money, just a little. To play only to win is for children. Don't you agree?"

"Yes, I agree," I nodded with a laugh. "They must have had problems with gambling sometime, so they set up the rules."

"So I think this is true. Not to gamble or drink give us time to rest when we stay longer in one place. We can talk more. Some of the people are very thoughtful and we have what we call philosophical discussions. So I think this helps me. Father Mary tried to help me talk about the eruption, but I was too sick to talk to him. These people are as good as Father Mary in talking to me. You were better than Father Mary who wanted to make me live like a saint because I survived. So you gave me the will to go on as a person, an ordinary person, not a saint, not somebody special only somebody with great luck. Talking to you healed me in my mind as much as Marie healed my body."

"I don't think so. I disagree. I think Marie kept both of us alive. I did not keep you alive." I could not take credit for either of us surviving.

"Yes, you did. I was not the same person I was before the eruption. You did not treat me like a different person, because you did not know me before. You also didn't treat me like what I am here, an oddity.

"So I still have things to sort out and these people help me. I do not think I will go back to my island. I think I will go to another one. It will be very similar, and very familiar, but it will not be a place of memory. I do not even know how long I stay with the circus. I may go back just when I have the money for the boat. I don't need more than that. I would not know what to do with more money. What has happened to you in this time, my friend?"

"I married the blonde lady that the wise woman predicted." I replied with a smile. "I changed jobs like she predicted, but I do not spend all of my time there. As I told you I am learning about plants. If I can't get someone else interested, I mean a physician; I am going to have to do it myself. I have been very busy and happy. Everything is better for me."

"Well, my friend, you do not have to set up or tear down tents in terrible weather, so everything should be better for you. One thing is better for me, besides the circus and the money for my boat. I found part of my family alive and well."

"I'm happy to hear that, Louis. Now maybe you don't feel so alone? Who did you find?"

"Some cousins. So it is better to have them than to have lost everything and everyone," Louis agreed with a nod of his head and a thin smile.

"Louis, I can tell there is a great deal more for us to talk about. Do you have time to go with me for a drink? Away from the circus so you don't get in trouble. The rum here is not as good as what you know. It is not like clairin I am sure, but I would like to buy you one of our rum drinks."

"I would like that. First I have to find the damned shoes and put them on."

Louis searched for his shoes and socks and finally found them thrust well back under his bed - put there with considerable distaste I imagine.

"I see why you have to wear these awful shoes on your feet, but I do not like it," said Louis sourly as he put his socks and shoes on. "You know Edward, you were right about the meaning of life. At least from what I have learned so far."

"I don't remember telling you anything about the meaning of life."

"So you forgot? You told me what you thought the meaning of life was, then you forget?"

"Yes, Louis, I forgot and I would like to know. What is the meaning of life?"

"You told me that people do the best they can to get through life comfortably. I think that is right. Besides that, I think I know that I can do things that I never thought I could do. Each day the memory of my loss is a little smaller. I get better and stronger."

"Today I might add a little to that knowledge of the meaning of life," I told him.

"Go on," Louis urged me.

"I would say that a life is worthwhile when a man gives more than he takes."

"Very good," Louis nodded in agreement. "So I also decided I do have debts to the people who died. I need to do the best that I can do, but I do not need to be an angel or a holy person. I need to live the kind of life they might have had if they lived. I need to have fun and laugh and cry. I need to do those ordinary things that people do. I need to try to keep each day special because each day is a gift to me that they don't have. Yet, I cannot be too goody-goody-goody about it. Do you know what I mean?"

"Not exactly."

"I am not a saint, Edward. I walk, see, hear, feel and think as well as ever. I have few remaining visible injuries, yet I do have scars inside. I learned that each day is valuable and single. So we never have a chance to live it again, but not everything we do is great or even near great. So we do the best we can. Do you understand now?"

"I'm beginning to."

"So you see, we have the day and we can waste it, or do the best we can with it. At the end of the day it is over and gone forever, the sun comes up for the next day not the old one. So we should be sure that we have no grief for the way the day we had was spent. Now do you understand better, Edward?"

"Yes, thank you, Louis. I don't remember exactly what I said, but I'm glad you did and are able to remind me."

"So I am a better philosopher because I remember good. I also learned something else. The saddest part was saying goodbye to trusting life was good and fair. I know the world is not a safe place and never was. Also, I know now I am a survivor, but tell me, Edward my friend, what do you think a survivor is?"

"A survivor is someone who remains alive, who lives on, who continues to function and prosper. A survivor is someone who remains alive after the death of others around him. Someone who endures after a disaster. You are a survivor because you are alive."

"Edward, I have come to believe there is more to it than what you have just said. Did we both walk away from an accident?"

"Yes, we did."

"Did we make changes in our lives?"

"Yes, Louis, we did that also."

Louis clapped me on the shoulder. "So from what we are discussing, I would say that many men are survivors even if they don't recognize themselves. Being a survivor does not require a catastrophic disaster that kills many people. I am a survivor and so, my friend, are you."

"Louis, let's go and have that drink. A friend told me of a place where we can be comfortable talking, then I will take you home to meet my wife. There are many things I haven't told her. I want her to see you and talk to you, then maybe she will understand why I want so badly to learn about plants. She is a good woman and is not so ordinary that she will not understand how amazing you are. Besides,

we have much more to say to each other."

C.M.F. Kosai

AFTERWORD

The eruption of Mont Pelee, Thursday morning, May 8, 1902, destroyed the city of St. Pierre, Martinique, French West Indies. It has since been rebuilt.

Father Mary, priest of Morne Rouge, died in a hospital in Fort-de-France, on September 1, 1902, the result of burns received two days earlier in another eruption of Mt. Pelee.

Louis Auguste Ciparis died in Panama in 1929, penniless and alone. He was also known as Louis Ciparis or Cyparis and Ludgar Sylbaris. He was born in 1874 at Precheur, Martinique, to Augusta Doreur and Eucher Sylbaris.

C.M.F. Kosai

ABOUT THE AUTHOR

An elementary school text reported a horrendous eruption that killed an entire city population, *except* one person. How provoking! Who was the survivor? How did this person survive? What happened to everyone else in the city? The first book source the author found said the survivor was a murderer waiting in this cell and watching the scaffold construction. Was this true?

The author, now far beyond elementary school days, lives in the comfort and beauty of Southern California, near Santa Barbara. Having written for newspapers and magazines while living in Spokane, Washington; Pasadena, California; Croton-on-Hudson, New York, and back to California. Age, education and skill finally brought answers found in *Surviving*. This authors' first book answers questions.

Printed in the United States
17595LVS00005B/163-225